EVE

IN

HOLLYWOOD

Also by Amor Towles

RULES OF CIVILITY

A GENTLEMAN IN MOSCOW

EVE
IN
HOLLYWOOD

Amor Towles

Copyright © Amor Towles, 2013

Cover illustration from the painting "Hitchcock Blonde" by New York City artist Duncan Hannah

FOR MY FATHER

He pushed his way through a tangle of briars, old flats and iron junk, skirting the skeleton of a Zeppelin, a bamboo stockade, an adobe fort, the wooden horse of Troy, a flight of baroque palace stairs that started in a bed of weeds and ended against the branches of an oak, part of the Fourteenth Street elevated station, a Dutch windmill, the bones of a dinosaur, the upper half of the Merrimac, a corner of a Mayan temple, until he finally reached the road. . . .

—*Nathanael West*, The Day of the Locust

EVE

IN

HOLLYWOOD

≡ CHARLIE ≡

IN THE DINING CAR, he was seated again at a table for four with the pretty young lady with the scar. She was reading that new detective story—the one with the strangled brunette on the cover. A page-turner, they called it, though you wouldn't know it from the pace that she was turning them. In all likelihood, she had just picked it up in the station to fend off friendly conversation. But he could understand that. Sometimes you just wanted to be left to yourself, even when it was for three thousand miles.

He nodded as he took the seat across from her. He put his napkin in his lap and looked out the window where the valley of the Rio Grande was giving way to the high, lonely deserts west of Exodus and east of John.

IN ANOTHER DAY, he'd be back in Los Angeles.

For the first half of the trip, he had put off thinking about what awaited him there. He had read the papers and sized up the passengers. In Kansas City, while they hitched a pair of Pullman cars from Memphis, Tennessee, he'd had a beer in the depot with a Wells Fargo man and almost missed the train.

But once they'd crossed into New Mexico, there was no more putting it off. He had to start giving it the attention it was due. In the days ahead, there'd be the selling of the house, the paying off of utilities, the closing of the account at the savings and loan. Every time he let his mind dwell on the list it grew longer. Selling his car. Packing his bags. Cleaning out that little storage space over the hallway that he hadn't visited since they'd stopped putting ornaments on the Christmas tree back in 1934. And then there was the list within the list: tending at long last to Betty's things. Her summer dresses, her aprons. Her hairbrush and brooches. Her Sunday service hats. The cookie cutters and rolling pins and pie plates that she had valued over everything else. To whom do you give a rolling pin, when every grown woman has a rolling pin of her own?

A good son, Tom had offered to travel out from Tenafly to help. And he had almost accepted his son's offer. That's how daunting it all seemed. But this was something he had to see to himself. Retired, widowed, moving back east to live with his boy, it was probably one of the last things he *would* see to himself.

ON THE OTHER SIDE of the window, the wide, cracked terrain of the Navajo reached to the horizon, ruthless and red. On his way east, he had been impressed by the buttes. Fixed against the sky, they seemed the ultimate survivors—outlasters of time and intent—as solitary and majestic as anything known to man. He had looked forward to passing back through this country, so that he could study them again. But as the train rushed on, he realized that they had become a blur. Without being conscious of it, he had let them recede from his field of vision so that he could consider the young lady's reflection in the window instead.

He first had seen her on the platform in New York—smoking a cigarette, with a small red valise at her feet. Fine-figured with sandy hair, elegant and self-possessed, she was hard to miss even in a crowd. Perhaps, especially in a crowd. He had taken a step to his right to get a better look, but the doors to the train had opened and she had disappeared among the others getting on.

What with finding his own compartment and securing his bag and making polite conversation with the shoe-leather salesman from Des Moines, he forgot altogether about the young lady with the red valise. Until the following morning when, as the train was nearing Chicago, he was seated at her table for breakfast.

She was gazing out the window and tapping the table with a brand-new pack of cigarettes. She didn't even look back to see who was joining her. But when the waiter offered to refill her cup, she turned just long enough to politely decline. And that's when he saw how her beauty had been marred.

He was surprised that he had missed it before. Because it had to be more than two inches long—running from the top of her cheekbone to the top of her chin. He had seen hundreds of them, of course. Star-shaped scars from a bludgeon to the brow; crescent-shaped scars from a knife on Encino; wide, white scars from fat-fingered stitch-ups in makeshift surgeries in the backs of garages. But those scars had all been on men, and they had been earned. Hunted. Almost longed for. With an inward shake of the head he turned to the menu and tried not to study the girl too closely, knowing that he would get a good look at her once she got up from the table.

But when the conductor passed down the aisle announcing the approach of Union Station, something interesting happened: Turning her gaze from the window, she called the conductor back and asked how much it would cost to extend her trip from Chicago to Los Angeles. Then, having paid the supplemental fare, she signaled the waiter for that refill, after all—as if she had just bought a ticket to the end of the line so that she could savor one more cup of coffee.

He had wondered a lot about that. It was one of those things he had wondered about in his berth at night while avoiding thoughts of what awaited him. Why would a young lady with a single valise who had boarded a train alone in New York suddenly extend her ticket from Chicago to L.A.? It's not as if she had received an urgent communication. Nor had she seemed particularly anxious when the conductor had called the next stop. But one thing was for certain: the decision had pleased her. Once her cup had been refilled, she leaned back with a sparkle in her eye that would have been the envy of any blonde in Brentwood.

ON THIS MORNING, as he was cutting into his ham and eggs across from the young lady with the scar, two women in their thirties took the empty seats at the table. Both were wearing those pillbox hats with the little black veils that are too small to veil anything. Their clothes were nicely made, but they were made for women in their fifties. The one in the blue hat sat on the other side of the table with a Presbyterian posture, and the one in the red hat sat at his side with her purse clasped tightly in her lap. They were from somewhere east of the Mississippi, he suspected, though not too far east. Maybe Cleveland.

—Good morning, they said.

—Good morning, he replied.

The young lady with the scar read on.

—Good morning, the woman in the blue hat repeated with a polite insistence that placed her a little closer to St. Louis.

—*Guten tag*, the young lady said without looking up from her book.

The woman in the blue hat raised her eyebrows for the benefit of her companion.

After the waiter had taken their order, the woman in the blue hat produced a small diary and began reviewing their itinerary: when they'd be arriving, where they'd be staying, a restaurant near the hotel that, according to a reliable friend, was clean and reasonably priced. There were also some recommendations as to where one shouldn't go and what one shouldn't do. He could tell it was a conversation that they had had before. They were going to have it every day until they were home again.

When the food came, the woman in the blue hat again raised her eyebrows for the benefit of her companion, this time to signify the rather rough delivery of the plates by the waiter.

As they ate, the woman in the blue hat was reminded of something she had recently heard and the conversation turned to the business of neighbors. The woman with the red hat listened with an air of having heard it all before and yet not wanting to miss a word. *It just shows to go you*, she would say, whenever a turn of events ratified her worst suspicions. Like when the colored boy who cared for the Adelsons' cars finally took their Cadillac for a night on the town. Or when young Miss Hollister followed that fast-talking schoolteacher all the way to Chicago, only to return Miss Hollister and child. And

Leonora Cunningham? After buying the Obermeyers' place in Clayton, and telling everyone who would listen about this curtain and that curtain and this lamp and that lamp, the bank examiners paid a visit to her husband's office and emerged with seven years of ledgers in a cardboard box!

Well. It just shows to go you.

He crossed his knife and fork on his plate and turned to the window, feeling a certain pang. It was the sort of pang that would strike him every now and then in the moments before some memory of Betty would surface. But no memory of his wife surfaced now. It was Caroline that he found himself thinking on.

When his son had first courted Caroline, he and Betty had been right proud. It wasn't because she was a college girl and the daughter of a New York attorney. Or, it wasn't only because of those things. It was because she had been so blue-eyed and bright. Sitting on their porch, she'd been ablush with talk of travel and music and books and all manner of open-endedness. But just six years later, she couldn't hide a hint of impatience. Like when Tom spoke of how much he enjoyed his position at his firm; or when he showed satisfaction in some little aspect of their house. And when she described a visit to an old friend in Greenwich, she twice told Tom that he wouldn't believe the trees in her backyard—as if the trees in Greenwich had been planted by a grander divinity than had the trees in Tenafly.

He had received his own serving of it too. On his first evening there, when he had told some old story from his days on the job, she had cut him short. It wasn't proper conversation for the dinner table, she had said. It wasn't proper conversation in front of the child. And the next day, when he had come downstairs for breakfast in his old gray suit, she cast him a glance suggesting that somehow his old gray suit wasn't proper either.

Caroline had itineraries and recommendations of her own, he thought to himself a little sadly. But it wasn't a trip to California that she was planning—it was her life.

AND YET, EVEN AS this thought was taking shape, he chastised himself for having it. He chastised himself as Betty would have.

After all, hadn't Caroline every right to plan her life? To imagine it? Hadn't he and Betty done just the same in their time? Hadn't they spent sweet evenings in that little place on Finley Avenue picturing themselves in one of the houses on Amesbury Road? Hadn't they spent some of the best years of their lives imagining a future for their boy, even before he could imagine a future for himself?

It was the American way.

Maybe it was the way all over the world.

In the reflection of the window, he tried to size himself up. He tried to size himself up the way that Caroline had—when he had sat down to breakfast in his old gray suit. In truth, he must have lost twenty pounds since Betty died. The weight had come right off his chest and arms. So now his old grey friend hung loosely on his frame, as if he had bought it second-hand. And what was he still wearing it for anyway? Where was he all suited up to go?

Well he knew that in this country, in this life, we fashion ourselves. We pick our spot and our companions and how we'll earn our keep, and that's how we go about the fashioning. Through the where of it, and the who, and the how. But if that is how we fashion ourselves, then surely it follows that with the loss of each of these elements comes the winnowing away. The burying of one's spouse, the retirement from the job, the moving from one's home where one has lived for twenty-two years—this is the undoing, the unmaking. It is through this process that time and intent reclaim the solitary soul for its grander purpose.

A humbling reminder, outside the window a telegraph wire supported by lean gray poles ran through the desert bearing news of weddings and wars.

That first night back east—when Caroline had cut him off in the middle of one of his old stories—even as his prideful self felt slighted, he knew that she was perfectly right. She was perfectly right to cut him off. Not because his stories were improper for the table, or improper for the child. But because they were an old man's stories. They were sorry and tired and over-told.

The vanity of vanities.

For there is no remembrance of former things. And neither shall there be any remembrance of things that are to come by those that shall come after.

—Is it any good?

As the two women from St. Louis were paying the waiter, the young lady with the scar had looked up from her book to ask for her check, and the woman in the blue hat had made use of the opening.

—The book you're reading, she said. Is it any good?

From her tone, you could tell that she didn't expect it to be.

The young lady studied her for a moment. Then she put out her cigarette, smiled like a Southern belle, and replied with the accent to match.

—Oh, it's all right, I reckon . . . It's got all manner of

nouns and verbs. And adjectives too! But it's just not true to life. Why, when the hero is slipped a Mickey Finn in chapter twenty-two, he topples over in sixty seconds flat. But in chapter fourteen, when he gets shot in the belly, he makes it halfway across town on foot. And as for ess ee ex: Suffice it to say, there's barely a mention.

She shook her head in a manner that presumed mutual disbelief.

—Now, I'm all in favor of poetic license; but a peck on the cheek in this day and age simply tries one's reason.

—Oh! said the women in their hats.

And as they bristled down the aisle, the young lady with the scar licked her finger and turned the page.

For a few minutes, she read idly on; but something in the book seemed to give her pause. She looked out the window. Then, after searching through a small purse, she asked if she could borrow a pen or pencil. He took the pencil from his jacket pocket and handed it to her. She flipped to the back of the book and jotted something down. Then she returned the pencil looking satisfied with her efforts.

The dining car was nearly empty now. A few tables away, a mother scolded her freckle-faced boy for playing soldiers with the salts and peppers. At the table in the corner, a studious young man invested himself in a stack of books. While outside, the telegraph wire ran on and on and on.

—You're right about a Mickey, he found himself saying. On a man of average weight even a five-star Mickey Finn would need ten minutes to do its damage.

The young lady lowered her book in order to eye him over the pages.

—But a bullet, he said, that's another thing altogether.

She put her book on the table.

—In 1924, I worked with a man in Ventura who was shot in the eye. The bullet glanced off his skull and went out his ear. He drove himself fifteen miles to a county clinic and lived to tell the tale. But Eddie O'Donnell? He got shot by a girl not much older than you with a .22 caliber pistol.

He held his fingers apart to show her how small that pistol had been.

—She'd been harboring someone; I don't remember who. We were just going to ask a few questions, when she plucked the gun from her purse. She was shaking like a leaf. We told her not to do anything that she'd regret; but she just closed her eyes and shot Eddie in the leg. He couldn't believe it. *Would you get a load of that?* he said to me. But the bullet had split his femoral artery. And Eddie bled to death right there on the floor of the kitchenette.

He looked out the window for a moment, the thoughts of Eddie O'Donnell getting the better of him—getting the better of him, after all these years.

—There's just no telling with bullets, he said.

When he looked back, she was taking him in. She nodded a few times to show her consideration for his old partner. Then she stretched her hand across the table.

—I'm Evelyn Ross.

She had a fine grip.

—I'm Charlie Granger.

She took a new cigarette from the pack and lit it.

—So, what's your story, Charlie?

Then she pushed the pack across the table.

It was the first time a woman had offered him a cigarette in more than twenty years.

So what's your story? she had asked, and that's what Charlie told her.

He told her how he and Betty had come to Los Angeles with their baby boy back in 1905, after they'd seen the advert in the Chicago papers looking for experienced officers willing to relocate. And how, when they got off the train, the whole town looked like an outpost for the Pony Express.

He told her what she already knew—about the rise of the studios and the matinee idols, the mansions and grand hotels. But he told her about the other Los Angeles too. The one that had emerged from the dust right along side the glamorous one and that had grown just as fast, if not faster. The Los Angeles of flatfoots and grifters and ladies of the night; of the shysters and snappers and has-beens. That city within the city that had its own diners and cable cars, its own chapels and banks—that had its own fashioning of failure and folly, and of grace and integrity too.

When he realized he'd probably gone on too long, he apologized, but she just pushed her cigarettes back across the table. She asked him to tell her about his life on the force, and she listened as closely when he told her about the glamourless day-to-day as when he told her about the front-page felons. And when he told her about the Doheny Drowning, she just lit up with laughter.

She laughed like young ladies should laugh in kitchens and castles, in Hollywood and Tenafly, and everywhere else in the world.

When the dining car was finally empty—after the studious young man had lugged his labors back to his berth and the freckle-faced kid had deftly swept the change that his mother had left for the waiter into his blazer pocket—Evelyn said that she owed Charlie an apology.

—When you sat down, she said, you looked like a salesman who's traveled his route ten times too many, and I had every intention of ignoring you. But once you got started, Mr. Granger, I could've listened all the way to Timbuktu.

She patted the table once and stood.

—I guess it just shows to go you.

But as she began to walk away, he stayed her progress by reaching for her arm. She looked back and tilted her head.

—May I ask you a personal question, Miss Ross?

—Of course, she said.

—Why did you extend your ticket from Chicago to Los Angeles?

She showed a hint of surprise and then smiled.

—To be perfectly honest, I have no idea.

And he could see it again: that sparkle of having made the decision. A decision that was all the better for having no cause or impetus or subjugation to a grander scheme. And suddenly, Charlie knew that he wasn't going back to his son's.

The young lady didn't continue on immediately. She lingered for a moment, mulling some quandary of her own as the East grew ever eastward.

—May I ask you a personal question, Mr. Granger? she said at last.

—Of course.

—How does one make a five-star Mickey Finn?

≡ PRENTICE ≡

ON THE SIXTH OF OCTOBER, 1938, at the northeast corner of the swimming terrace of the Beverly Hills Hotel, Prentice Symmons stopped to catch his breath between two chaises longues. He stopped as had Kutozov on the fields of Borodino; as had Washington on the western shores of the Hudson having slipped through the grasp of Howe. Here on the swimming terrace, the sun paused in its course and the snap of the canopies subsided as Prentice leaned upon his cane.

In the limpid pool, a starlet swam alone. Her auburn hair was neatly tucked beneath a light blue cap, and her delicate arms parted the water's dappled surface without a sound. She was this fair city's newest nightingale. At the four corners of the pool stood cabana boys, each hoping that when she concluded her fiftieth lap she would climb from the water in his proximity so that he would have the honor of bestowing upon her a towel. Not ten years before, when this damsel (or rather, her predecessor) had finished her calisthenics, it would have been toward Prentice that she swam. Calling out some coy remark, she would have splashed him playfully from the pool's edge before backstroking into fame's embrace.

Alas, there is no fixing of man's position in the system of

the heavens, anymore than one can fix the position of a skiff at sea. Alas, yes, alas; but also, avanti!

—Afternoon, Mr. Symmons, said the boy at north northwest. It was James, the arch one. *Afternoon*, he said without a modifier while betraying the slightest smile, as if winking at some shared acknowledgment of Prentice's professional standing. It was a harbinger, no doubt, of the cad's inevitable successes as a talent agent, or felon.

—Good afternoon, Prentice corrected as he passed.

At the edge of the terrace awaited the twenty-six steps to the main floor. They knew as well as he that not a hundred feet away an elevator had lately been installed. But he had no intention of giving them the satisfaction of using it. He brandished his cane once and launched his ascent. Five, ten, fifteen, twenty. It is a good afternoon, he remarked to himself as he crested the top. His daily exercise had been completed, the insolence of the cabana boy parried, the twenty-six steps bested, and it was only half past three.

Back inside the hotel proper, he smiled when he passed the elegantly scripted sign that pointed the way to the lobby. To refer to that space as a *lobby* was to commit a crime of nomenclature. In such a room, did Kubla Khan hold court. It was a geographic pinpoint through which within the hour the world would come and go. Misguided financiers newly arrived from Manhattan with a single change of clothes would soon be signing the registry. Delivery boys would be appearing in the nick of time with indistinguishably altered dresses, or with flower arrangements composed like Elizabethan sonnets to express admiration or regret. And the town's young Turks on their way to the bar would pass the late-lunching Titans they aspired to supplant.

But as Prentice rounded the corner and passed between

the potted palms, the Fates once again laid claim to their supremacy, to their dominion over mortal men. For there, under the painted ceiling, a delicate beauty sat blithely in his chair—turning indifferently through the pages of *Gander*, the latest periodical dedicated to the rise and fall of the latest. One could hardly blame her for choosing his chair. It was an inviting chair, plush and well positioned. And she had no reason to know better.

He stole a glance around the room looking for the desk captain or concierge, both of whom were otherwise engaged. So, letting his eyebrows droop and leaning on his cane a tad more than necessary, he approached.

—Ahem.

Looking up from her periodical, the young woman, who had seemed such a delicate beauty from afar, revealed a scar on her face that could have marked the nemesis of Zorro! Her eyebrows rose with a poised curiosity. In the instant, he could see that there would be no appealing to sympathies. He resumed his upright posture.

—Pardon me for the intrusion, he ventured. But would it inconvenience you terribly to move to this other chair?

He pointed his cane lightly at the empty seat three feet to her left.

—My girth, you see, demands unusual quarter.

She tilted her head and smiled.

—But they are the same size . . .

He cleared his throat.

—Yes. So they are, so they are. And as such, I daresay I could presumably *fit* in this empty chair. But you see, I am afraid . . . How does one put it . . . ? It is not *my* chair.

She laid her magazine in her lap and sat back, as if to say that she was ready to hear his case with unwavering attention.

God bless her!

He adopted the bearing of Cicero.

—Young lady, he began, though I have stayed in this hotel without interruption for more than one thousand nights, that should not give me claim to special privileges in the lobby. Were you to spend but a single night in the hotel, you would have every right to expect all of its graces. So, I will not appeal to your sense of propriety. What I must appeal to instead is your sense of *forbearance*. For I am quite simply an aging, overweight oncewas who no longer lays claim to his city's storied indulgences—other, that is, than to invest the four o'clock hour observing the Turn of the Wheel from this my Elba . . . my fence post . . . my perch.

The young woman smiled delightfully and shifted to the adjoining chair.

—You are a woman of great courtesy, Prentice said with a bow.

—Hardly, she replied. But I've got a soft spot for oncewases.

EXEMPLIFYING THE GRACE of the well bred, the young woman accepted Prentice's offer to share a pot of tea and a plate of currant scones with clotted cream and jam.

—What brings you to California, my dear, Prentice asked as he filled her cup.

—I'm not sure. I suppose I was in the mood for a bit of adventure.

—Well, you have come to the right place. Teddy Roosevelt and Ernest Hemingway traveled all the way to Africa to see the creatures of the wild; to join in the hunt and put themselves in mortal danger. I tell you, they need only have come to this lobby.

The young woman laughed.

It was a marvelous laugh.

—Mortal danger . . . ? she queried.

—I do not exaggerate. In the coming minutes, you will see predators dressed in coats of fur as thick as an ocelot's. In the high grass around the watering hole, you will see conniving dogs lying in wait for the approach of young, unguarded gazelles. And every day at five, there is a stampede.

She laughed again, and he smiled to hear it.

There was nothing jaded or ugly about her laughter. On the contrary, it was the laugh of one who knows well the foibles of others without begrudging them. It was a tribute to the human comedy—the sort of laugh he had not heard in years, or maybe eons. The sort of laugh that should not be interrupted!

(A waiter approaching with a plate of tea sandwiches is discreetly waved off.)

And what a refined sense of curiosity she exhibited in her questions. It was a curiosity one might have imagined in the young Galileo or Isaac Newton. Without a slavish adherence to the faddish certainties of yesteryears (in fact, with an instinctive suspicion of them), she had an interest in the *world*—and those invisible, immutable laws that actually spin it on its axis and keep us all from flinging into space.

So, leaving a history of Spanish missionaries and the great migration spawned by Sutter's Mill to other professors, he told her instead of the founding of Beverly Hills. A desert within a desert, Beverly Hills had lain fallow for a thousand years until Pioneer Oil arrived and drilled deep into the ground in search of petrol only to discover . . . water—that tasteless, shapeless, colorless substance without which, nothing.

(Prentice gestured to the periphery, indicating by general

reference the orange blossoms and honeysuckle that abounded just outside the lobby's walls.)

Then he described for her how in 1912 the Andersons secured these ten acres with a million dollars and a dream—a dream to build amidst gardens and bowers, a temporary residence par excellence. And vision had led to vision. For within the hotel's walls had been imagined Caribbean battles between privateers and His Majesty's fleet; the coldhearted dalliances of latter-day Cleopatras; and the all-encompassing charity of a bowler-hatted tramp.

—Why, not a hundred feet from here Chaplin, Fairbanks, Pickford, and Griffith struck the anvil of artistic independence to forge United Artists!

Etc., etc., etc.

Unexpectedly, the young woman repaid him in kind with one of the most fantastic tales of Hollywood that he had ever heard—one that she had learned in the dining car of the Golden State Limited from a homicide detective, no less. And when she stood to go, he roused himself from his chair without his cane in order to take her hand and thank her for a delightful afternoon.

PRENTICE'S ORIGINAL PLAN THAT DAY had been to dwell for the hour after tea in the pages of the Lambs' *Tales from Shakespeare*. But having completed his daily exercise, waved off sandwiches, and conversed at length with a lovely young woman, when he finally rose to leave the lobby, he felt a sense of élan.

Why rush back to one's quarters, he thought? Mr. & Mrs. Lamb were as genteel and sympathetic as any companions known to man. They would be the first to understand the cause of his delay. And with that, he headed out the lobby doors into the aromatic air as an autumnal dusk prepared to shroud the Hollywood Hills.

Edgar, the bell captain, was patting the roof of a taxicab having helped a guest into the backseat. When he turned to find Prentice before him, he snapped to attention.

—Mr. Symmons!

—Hello, Edgar. How are things?

—I'd say it's shaping up to be a beautiful evening.

—I think you're right, Edgar. In fact, it seems a perfect night to dine at *Maison Robert*. Could you see if William is free?

—Yes, sir, Edgar said with verve before jogging off to the lower lot.

Maison Robert . . . , thought Prentice with the smile of anticipation (as he crossed the drive to the large Tuscan pots where the gardenia bushes bloomed). How excited they would be to see him. Without mention of the months that had passed, and without a glance at *The Book*, Robert himself would lead Prentice to his old banquette. After cold asparagus soup, Prentice would have the porterhouse steak, potatoes dauphinoise, and a soufflé. Or better yet . . . When the waiter came for his order, Prentice would say: It is up to Bertrand! And when the last morsel had been picked from his plate, he would step once again through the kitchen's swinging doors to proclaim the only word that applied: *magnifique.*

But as he was bending down to savor the smell of the blossoms, he heard the turn of an ignition and looked back to see a black sedan, which had been parked at the end of the drive, slowly rolling forward.

His heartbeat quickened.

He was a hundred feet from the lobby door, and no one was about. The sedan continued to advance at its ominous pace.

Then, in the very moment its engines began to race, a man and woman appeared from the other direction on foot. It was the Sandersons—the fine young couple from Houston who were celebrating their fifth anniversary. They must have just taken an evening stroll among the roses in Municipal Park before returning to dress for dinner.

As they approached the lobby, they gave Prentice a warm Texas greeting and, for the moment, the sedan's engines idled. For the moment.

—Wait! Prentice called to the Sandersons. Wait a second, if you would. I was just headed inside myself. Allow me to accompany you.

On the following afternoon when Prentice arrived in the lobby for tea, he was delighted to find the young woman with the scar awaiting him. Her name was Evelyn Ross, lately of Manhattan. When he formally introduced himself, she sat back with a look of self-recrimination, then simply said:

—Of course.

Now, having lived in Hollywood for nearly half his life, Prentice Symmons was well acquainted with the feigning of recognition. He was neither insulted by it, nor did he take it too closely to his flattered heart. Rather, he completed the charade by smiling and nodding in the fatuous manner of faded celebrity with the full expectation that the conversation could quickly shift toward politics or other forms of weather.

But Miss Ross commenced to recall six different films in which he had appeared. By her own admission, she had been sneaking into movie houses since the age of thirteen! And to her lasting credit, she recalled his career as one who plays a game of memory, rather than one who has been presented the opportunity to fawn. With the occasional tap of a finger to her lip, she reconstructed scenes that he had stolen; she rehashed outrageous twists of plot; and she rekindled romances that never had any business being doused. So complete was her inventory that they both fell silent once she was done.

Did he miss it? she asked at last. Did he miss the silver screen?

—Pah, he said with a wave of the hand.

What he missed was *the stage.*

—For the viewer, Evelyn—for the sales girl or senator, for the rogue or Rothschild—the cinema is the ultimate entertainment. It is an overflowing font of romance and danger. But for the performer, the romance and danger reside on the stage. When shooting a close-up, the movie camera must have you to itself. Thus, when you perform the most charged of cinematic scenes, you are likely to deliver your lines alone. *Lady, by yonder blessed moon I swear . . .* Or so you proclaim to the cold, black eye of the camera before being excused to your dressing room, so that Juliet can implore in your absence that you *Swear not by the moon, th' inconstant moon . . .* Wherefore art thou Romeo, indeed!

Prentice paused briefly to serve the tea before it oversteeped.

—But on stage, my dear, on stage it is in the very interstice between the full-blooded physical forms of the actor and actress that the spark is struck. It is in that space between two gazes which search each other out, between two fingertips which nearly touch . . . And danger? For the actor, every dram of it is in the theater. Not because of crocodiles and sabers, you understand, but because the edge of the stage is a precipice! For there are no takes in the theater, Evelyn; no second chances. One false move, and the actor plummets through the pitch toward the craggy bottom of his own self-indictments.

Her appreciation for his argument almost instinctual, Evelyn's cheeks betrayed a rosy flush.

—Then why, she asked almost breathlessly, why did you stop acting?

—You're sweet, my dear.

But in her perplexity, she seemed genuine. Genuine!

—My rotundity, he explained.

And before she could express her shock (or God forbid, her sympathy), he raised a stalling hand.

—Don't pity me for it. Are there elements of stardom that I miss? Why, there are elements of boarding school that I miss. There are elements of my most catastrophic romances that I miss. So let us agree, that missing is not at the heart of the matter.

AT THE TOLL OF ONE in the morning, the lobby of the Beverly Hills Hotel had been empty for almost an hour. There were no more guests checking in; no gilded affairs dispersing. Through the doors of the bar drifted the tinkling of piano keys at the hands of a capable straggler who had presumably been thrown from his apartment and who now finally slumbered, having made the G Major 7 with his head. While behind the desk, the night clerk Michael stood alone, fending off sleep.

Under the circumstances, it was quite natural for him to welcome a chance to chat.

So, after marveling at the business of the season, and remarking on a handful of recent arrivals, Prentice and Michael agreed that Miss Ross was a delightful young woman. But from where and when and how did she arrive? Well, it seems that she arrived by taxicab from the railway with a single red valise. And was she here to see old friends? It was hard to say, for she had placed no phone calls and received no visitors. On her first night, she did entrust two items of jewelry to the hotel safe: a sizable engagement ring and a diamond earring without its pair; although (as Michael noted sotto voce), on the very next morning, she had taken the earring from the safe and returned in the late afternoon with a selection of dresses and three pairs of shoes.

An excellent use of a young woman's wherewithal, the two gentlemen agreed.

Prentice wondered out loud if she was the same Miss Ross, friend of a friend, who lived on Gramercy Park . . . ?

No, replied Michael, turning the registration card so that Prentice could read.

—Ah, Prentice said. Well. Goodnight, my fine fellow.

Then he ambled down the hall with a smile on his lips. For Miss Evelyn Ross, lately of Manhattan, had apparently resided at 87 East 42nd Street. Or, as it is more commonly known: Grand Central Station.

At room 102 he put his key in the door, eager to cast off his shoes and recline with a square of Spanish chocolate and the pages of Mr. & Mrs. Lamb. But as his door closed behind him, his heart skipped a beat. Across the sitting room, a curtain billowed once before the open terrace door. For a minute Prentice stood stock-still under the grip of his accelerating pulse. He considered backing into the hallway and dialing the house phone for security. But Devlin was on duty tonight, and Prentice had called him not two weeks before, only to suffer the humiliation of having empty closets opened one by one.

Prentice attempted to steel himself to the task.

—Who's there? he called out.

He moved sideways to spy into the bedroom and then eased open the door to the bath with his cane. After circling once and finding nothing out of place, he locked the terrace door and sat relieved on the edge of his bed. And that is when he saw it: There, between the turned down sheets and pillows, sat Mr. & Mrs. Lamb with an unfamiliar bookmark. With a tremble of the hand he opened the pages and felt a wave of nausea.

It had been a year since he had purged his room of memorabilia: the gaudy posters with their imperial fonts and faraway gazes; the playbills; the overtly staged studio stills; even the candids—like the shot of him and Garbo addled at Antonio's. Into boxes they had all been thrown, and sent to the hotel's cellar.

But here, marking the first page of *Hamlet*, was a ticket to the premiere of his acclaimed run as the Danish Prince at the Old Vic in 1917.

Prentice Symmons slid from his bed to the floor and wept.

PRENTICE SPENT MUCH of the following day in his room. When he woke, he neither showered nor shaved. When his regular breakfast was served, he left half the potatoes uneaten beside the remnants of egg and did not ring for the service to be cleared. He sat on the couch in his robe as the room filled with the odor of the unfinished breakfast and as the minutes dismantled the hours. In the early afternoon, he heard the chambermaids knocking on doors and pushing their linen-laden trollies. When they knocked upon his, he fully intended to call out that they were not needed. But when he heard Bridie's voice, from some force of habit he invited her in.

A professional young Irish woman and mother of six, Bridie did not display the slightest surprise to find Prentice in his robe. But within the instant she had whisked his plates into the hall, drawn the curtains, and cracked the terrace window to admit fresh air. When she went into the bedroom, he watched her through the open door. He watched as she returned his shoes and jacket to their closet. He watched as she made the bed with efficiency and care, snapping the fresh sheets and tucking them tightly into place. He watched as she rinsed his unused shaving brush and hung it on its golden hook to dry. And when she had finished, he roused himself from the couch and thanked her as one who thanks a chance apostle for the telling of a timely parable. For if one is to maintain the slightest hint of pride, his curtains must be drawn, his bed made, and his clothes put away.

It was after three o'clock.

He bathed and dressed in a three-piece suit with a well-wound watch in his vest and set out for tea. Evelyn did not appear, but she had been kind enough to leave a note of regret on his chair and a promise to see him anon. This unnecessary gesture (coming in concert with the rare treat of cranberry scones) completed the revival of his spirits. And it was this revival, no doubt, that led him to play the part of a fool.

For when his tea had been cleared, Prentice happened to notice that lingering by the front desk was a certain actor-of-the-moment—an actor whom as a younger man had played a supporting role in one of Prentice's finest films. And rather than keeping his counsel, Prentice strolled across the lobby with his cane in hand, calling out the actor's name.

Exhibiting a touch of surprise, the actor remarked how pleasant it was to see Prentice. Then he made a friendly inquiry into Prentice's welfare (an inquiry that is best met with a generous affirmation and the word adieu). But in his elevated spirits, Prentice leaned upon his cane and began to harken back; at which point, this actor-of-the-moment played the part of someone who had forgotten his billfold in his car, stranding Prentice in the lobby with his days of yore.

At the front desk, it was evident from the attention that Simone and Christopher paid to the shuffling of papers that they had heard every word—as had the young socialite who stood by the elevator doors with her dog.

Prentice felt his face grow flush.

—I am expecting a telegram, he heard himself proclaiming to Simone, in the manner of one for whom telegrams urgently arrive. When it appears, send it to the pool!

As PRENTICE PASSED the elegantly scripted sign that pointed the way to the pool, he unleashed a spate of acrimony—not toward his old supporting cast member, but rather toward himself. For what had he expected? To be embraced and invited for supper? So that they could speak of olden times—when their positions were reversed? At the peak of his fame, had not Prentice been strolled upon and cornered in lobbies by fading acquaintances? And had he not performed stage-left exits of his own?

Having descended the twenty-six steps at too quick a pace, Prentice found that he needed to catch his breath, so he headed toward a chair at the pool's edge. Gratefully, the terrace was empty. The cool October air had driven the starlets and cabana boys into their respective retreats.

But just as Prentice was about to reach his chosen chair, from the corner of his eye he glimpsed a figure slip behind a hedge. Feeling his heart rate leap, Prentice bypassed the chair and made for the rear gate. But the shadow, having deftly crossed the terrace, now ducked behind an adjacent cabana. In a state of panic, Prentice looked for a fellow guest or chambermaid, and failed to see the ice tea table directly in his path. He tripped and fell to his knees. The force of impact tore his pant leg. He began to heave, knowing that above all else, he must regain his footing. With a flash of single-mindedness, he stood to his full height, but the terrace wheeled around him. And when upon the breeze he heard the whispering of his name, Prentice Symmons finally acknowledged the unacknowledgable—that it was time.

On this day, on this terrace, at this Trafalgar, they would meet. Without the exchange of a word, a single hand would extend into space and topple Prentice into the pool of the Beverly Hills Hotel where, hapless, he would thrash for a sliver of eternity, before sinking at last to the depths.

Oh, fateful day.

Oh, ignominious—

—Prentice?

A gentle hand took hold of his elbow.

—Evelyn, he gasped.

—Jesus, Prentice. You're white as ghost. Are you all right?

—Ohhh, he moaned from the bottom of his soul; and then began to sob.

She led him to a chaise. She sat at his side and took his hands in her own to still them from trembling.

—What is it, Prentice? What's happened?

—Evelyn. He was almost upon me.

—Who?

—Like a minion of the devil, he's haunted me. Hunted me. Waiting for the perfect moment to bring me to my end.

—Who, Prentice?

—A shadow.

—What shadow?

Silence fell around them. A silence as unvaultable as time. The silence from which all things spring, all things good and evil. With a great effort, Prentice raised his gaze and looked her in the eyes.

—The shadow of my former self.

It was a pitiful admission. A *comic* one. It had been written in the pages of Prentice's personal history to elicit guffaws. But young Evelyn, so prone to beautiful laughter, remained sober. Sympathetic. Unflinching.

—In 1936, Prentice confessed, on a crowded avenue he shoved me in front of a tram. And last New Year's Eve, he nearly succeeded in throwing me from my own balcony to the flagstones below. That is why I moved to the first floor.

—But why, Prentice?

Casting his gaze downward again, he saw that she was still holding his hands. And he could feel how her innermost temperature was transferring itself through his skin and coursing through his veins, bringing warmth to his core in the manner of a potent drink. And in this state of intoxication, the words spilled forth: how it all began, even as a boy at his grandmother's; lemon squares with a shortbread crust and a bright yellow curd; the bacon sandwiches, so fatty and savory and divine; and later, the ingenuity of the profiterole!

Ah, the very shame of it.

He told her too, how he had learned to hold it in check during all those promising years—first, as a lineless lord-officer-soldier-attendant; then, as an understudy in the wings mouthing monologues word-for-word; and at last, as the leading man with a rapier in his left hand and a pistol in his right. But with every step toward success, he had advanced as well toward a darker humor. He became surly. Impatient. Abrupt.

—Do you know what I was doing, Evelyn, at the height of my stardom? Can you even imagine? I was starving! Over the years, I convinced myself that I had built worthy defenses—a fortress against my weakness. But on the Ides of March, 1935, left alone by Lucifer in a lavish hall where the press had yet to arrive, my fortitude failed me. On that day, I gorged. I gorged on honey baked ham and linzer torte and strawberries dipped in cream. It was my crossing of the Rubicon, Evelyn. In the days that followed, I tumbled down the vertiginous trail of my frailty. Head over heels I fell; and as I passed the olive trees jutting from the jagged hills, not once did I reach for a branch.

In hearing this, Evelyn's eyes grew brighter with every word. She did not look disgusted or shocked. She looked defiant!

—I want you to listen to me, Prentice, she said in the manner of one who has slayed a dragon of her own. I want you to listen very carefully. Are you listening, Prentice?

—Yes, Evelyn.

—Since that day, since that day with the ham and the torte, have you been surly, impatient, or abrupt?

Prentice raised his head.

—Not for a minute.

She patted him on the back of the hand.

—Exactly.

Her expression relaxed. They sat holding hands. And as the sky turned indigo, a waxing moon rose over the hotel, giving the entire setting the look of the desert oasis it was.

—Evelyn . . .

—Yes, Prentice.

—I must admit to something else.

He shifted on the seat so that he could face her.

—I have lied to you.

She did not look offended or surprised.

—In what way? she asked.

—About the lobby.

She offered a bemused smile.

—No. I am serious, Evelyn. Deadly serious. I have encouraged you to take up residence beside me in the lobby, calling it the world. But it isn't the world. It isn't a continent, or a country, or a town. It isn't even a room! It is a prison cell. It is my Bastille.

For the first time in years, Prentice felt the force of his own convictions.

—Providence has sent you to Los Angeles, Evelyn. And you must visit with It. Young William, one of the hotel's drivers, has been put at my disposal; I put him at yours. You must go out into the scent of the orange blossoms, out into the temperate nights of Hollywood where all its most elusive delicacies hide in plain sight. Go tonight. Start by dining on the Sunset Strip at Antonio's on osso buco with risotto Milanese!

—We can go together.

(So suggested Evelyn, sweet Evelyn.)

—No, said Prentice, rising to his feet. You must go without me, *mon ami*. For tonight upon the platform, before the crow of the cock, I have an appointment with an apparition.

═ OLIVIA ═

WHEN OLIVIA HAD almost run out of questions about track and field, she excused herself politely from the table for two.

Given the choice, she would have preferred to be on the little bedroom terrace that she hardly ever used. Bounded by white stucco, climbing with ivy, and bordered by love-in-idleness, it seemed the perfect grotto for the weary in waiting. But as she passed a neighboring table, she paused to accept and return the compliment from the comedian; and at the booth a few steps beyond, she told the director with the Slavic accent that she would very much enjoy having the opportunity to work with him as well. She tucked a curl behind an ear, offered a delicate smile, and continued toward the powder room hoping to find it empty.

But of course, it wasn't.

They hardly ever were.

LEANING AGAINST THE WALL by the sinks was the rather rough looking blonde whom Olivia had noticed dining alone at the bar. She was smoking a cigarette and listening to the attendant who was describing a night on the town as she aimlessly wiped the countertop. Miguel, the girl was saying, had borrowed his uncle's car and dressed in a three-piece suit. He had taken her dancing at a little club on Shepherd Avenue. A club that had the finest band en Los Ángeles . . . En California . . . En todo el—

The girl stopped short when she saw Olivia's reflection in the mirror. She apologized and retreated to the back of the room where she began folding and refolding hand towels. Olivia approached a sink and turned on the faucets. The blonde didn't move. She closed her eyes and rested her head against the wall, as if she could hear the rumba of the girl's reminiscence.

From across the restaurant, Olivia had imagined that the blonde was in that league of callous women who began their workday at the bars of the Hollywood restaurants and hotels. But from up close, Olivia could see how terribly off the mark she had been. In the mirror's reflection, the blonde's unscarred profile suggested an almost aristocratic beauty with no hint of an ugly enterprise's toll. And she had the effortless poise of a woman raised in privilege. With her arm hanging gracefully at her side, her fingers slender and unadorned, she held her cigarette at an upward angle so that the smoke could spiral toward the ceiling with an enviable lack of purpose.

—Would you like one?

Olivia looked up to find that the blonde had caught her staring.

—Why yes, thank you, she replied, though she hadn't smoked in more than a year.

The blonde slid the pack across the vanity.

Olivia took one of the cigarettes and lit it. She leaned against the wall, assuming the blonde would make conversation, but she didn't.

When Olivia inhaled, the taste of the smoke brought back foolish memories . . . of hiding with her sister behind an elm tree in Saratoga with pilfered cigarettes and a pack of cinnamon gum. They were memories from another season—a season when the two of them had shared clothes and secrets and sly remarks.

How never-resting time does lead summer on . . .

—So, is he as boring as he seems?

—I'm sorry? asked Olivia.

—Your date, said the blonde. Isn't he the one who wears the big white hats?

Olivia laughed.

—Wilmot's not a date. It's more of a work dinner. But yes, I suppose he is the one who wears the big white hats.

—Well, every time he squints at the horizon, I fall asleep.

Olivia laughed again.

—I think they call it the strong and silent type.

—They can call it whatever they like. But from where I was sitting, he looked more like the go-on-and-on-and-on type. Do you ever get a word in edgewise?

Olivia extended her arm in an ironic flourish.

—*Give every man thine ear, but few thy voice . . .*

The blonde raised a questioning eyebrow.

—Shakespeare . . . , Olivia confessed. Courtesy of my mother.

—What else did your mother teach you?

Olivia considered.

—A lady never finishes a cigarette, a drink, or a meal.

The blonde nodded her head in a show of familiarity.

—My mother told me that it was more important to be interested than interesting.

—Have you heeded her advice?

—Only as a last resort.

Olivia and the blonde were both silent—reflecting for the moment on motherly advice and other monoliths. Then Olivia held up her cigarette to show that it had been half smoked and, with a smile of goodhearted resignation, she dutifully tamped it out.

As the waiter cleared Olivia's unfinished entrée, Wilmot was explaining the insignificance of the marathon when compared to the fifty-yard dash.

—A marathon is really a contest of endurance, he was saying, not of athleticism. You'll often see a topflight sprinter excel at a variety of sports, but a great marathoner will only excel at one. And there are whole miles in a marathon that have no bearing on victory. But I think we can safely say that in the fifty-yard dash, every footfall counts.

As Wilmot spoke, he rubbed the tablecloth with the flat of his hands. Back and forth they went in the spot where his plate had been, as if he'd been asked by the maître d' to keep the linens smooth. And Olivia realized that he didn't want to be there either. He too was fulfilling an obligation—playing his part in this orchestrated pair of Maid Marian and Wyatt Earp.

But that didn't mean he was about to ask for the check. When the waiter returned to inquire about dessert, Wyatt (with his white hat securely on his head) would presumably note how famous Antonio's was for its baked Alaska; and Marian would smile politely and say that baked Alaska sounded perfectly delicious. And they would spend another hour at this table for two talking of the shot put and the high jump and God knows what else before heading their separate ways.

The blonde from the powder room wouldn't stay for dessert, Olivia found herself thinking. But then, she probably wouldn't have put herself in this position in the first place. Having dined alone at the bar, she could now pay her check and go home to her own ivied terrace. Or more likely, head off in search of the finest band in Los Ángeles. En California. En todo el mundo.

—Cousin Livvy! Is that you?

Wyatt and Marian both looked up in surprise.

It was the blonde, but she looked bright-eyed and boisterous. And she had a Southern accent . . .

—It's me, Evvie! she said, placing her fingers to her chest. All the way from Baton Rouge!

—Evvie . . . , said Olivia, I didn't know that you were in town . . . .

—I'm here with Aunt Edith! She's waiting at the hotel, so I don't have a minute. But they'd just paddle me back home if we didn't catch up.

—Please join us, said Wilmot on his feet.

He brought a chair from the neighboring table and placed it between his and Olivia's.

—Oh no, chided Evvie. Boy girl, boy girl!

She picked up Wilmot's cocktail with both hands and placed it gently in front of the empty chair. Then she claimed his spot as the waiter arrived with a martini.

—In God We Trust, Evvie said, raising the glass.

—In God We Trust, Wilmot repeated a little uncertainly, as he raised his own.

—So . . . , said Olivia. What's the news from Baton Rouge . . . ?

—You wouldn't believe me if I told you, said Evvie. You remembah that colored boy who worked for Aunt Ethel? Well, last Septembah he up and drove off in Aunt Ethel's Cadillac—with Aunt Ethel in it! And when the police finally pulled them over in Kansas City, it was the colored boy who was in the passengah seat and Aunt Ethel behind the wheel.

—I do declayah, said Olivia.

Evvie turned to Wilmot confidentially.

—Aunt Ethel always had a fondness for oldah husbands; and youngah men . . .

Wilmot, who was smoothing the linens again, attempted to change the subject.

—Have you been in Los Angeles long, Evvie?

—Just a few weeks, she sighed. But it's been divine. Why, we've seen Charlie Chaplin's house and Lon Chaney's garage. We've been to the Tar Pits and the fights at the American Legion . . .

Wilmot blinked as Evvie spoke, as if he was having trouble keeping up.

—Some dessert? asked the waiter, who was leaning over the table with his pad and pen.

Wilmot looked up at the waiter as if he hadn't understood the question.

—I know just the thing, said Evvie. Let's have dessert in Santa Monica. I have it on good authority that until the stroke of midnight the finest donuts in all of Los Angeles are cooked on the Santa Monica piers. We can dangle our toes in the water and watch the casinos drift out to sea!

—I haven't had a donut in ten years, Olivia admitted.

—Well, that settles it.

The girls turned to Wilmot.

—I'm actually feeling a little under the weather, he confessed while mopping his brow with his pocket square.

—What is it, my dear? asked Evvie. Are you coming down with something?

—No. I'll be fine. I'm just going to sit here for a minute. Why don't you two girls go on without me.

When Evvie and Olivia put their napkins on the table, Wilmot looked almost relieved.

—Lovely to meet you, Evvie said, then she took Olivia by the hand.

Evvie tugged her past a screenwriter, a leading man, and the maître d'—anyone of whom might normally have waylaid her—and Livvie found herself giggling like a schoolgirl in the midst of a narrow escape.

Outside, the wind was wild. The fronds of the palm trees rattled overhead and dust spiraled off the sidewalk in little tornadoes.

—I hope that Wilmot will be alright, said Olivia.

—Oh, he'll be fine, said Evvie. He just disagreed with something he drank.

She slipped past the valets in order to survey the street. Halfway up the block what looked like a teenage boy in a chauffeur's uniform waved. He was standing in front of a forest green Packard.

—Is that yours? Olivia asked.

—A friend of a friend's. Come on.

And the two cousins made the twenty-yard dash for the car.

ONCE THEY WERE IN THE BACK of the Packard driving along Sunset, the blonde stuck out her hand and formally introduced herself. Then she instructed her driver to head for the Santa Monica piers.

—You were serious? asked Olivia.

—Absolutely. The donuts are the next item on the list. Isn't that right, Billy?

—Yes, ma'am!

—So, have you really been to all those other places?

—Well, not to Lon Chaney's garage. But we've been to the Tar Pits and the fights. We've been to the Wishing Chair at Forest Lawn Cemetery and the parade on Santa Claus Lane.

With one hand on the steering wheel and one eye on the road, Billy leaned to his right, took something from the glove compartment, and handed it into the backseat. It was a waiter's pad from the Beverly Hills Hotel. The fourth page was titled SIGHTS TO SEE BEFORE I LEAVE L.A. It had an itemized list of fifteen destinations, thirteen of which had been checked off in a forest green ink, as if the pen had come with the car.

Leaning over Olivia's shoulder, Eve pointed to item number fourteen: The Donuts of Santa Monica.

—How long have you been in Los Angeles? Olivia asked in disbelief.

Eve pretended to count on her fingertips.

—Two months, three weeks, and a day.

—I've been here for four years and haven't done half of these things.

—You've been busy.

Olivia took another look at the list.

—Skating?!

—The Pan Pacific Rink is one in a million! Billy enthused as he pulled himself up by the wheel. The real McCoy! Not only is it the largest skating rink in the world, every Saturday they have an orchestra that plays polkas and on Sundays they serve hot toddies!

Eve winked at Olivia.

—Speaking of hot toddies, Billy: What have we got in the glove?

Billy leaned to his right again and handed back a flask. Eve took a generous sample.

—Gin, she said like the pleasantly surprised.

But when she held out the flask, she could see that Olivia hesitated.

—Come on, Livvy. Even a churchbell's gotta swing, if it's gonna chime.

Olivia laughed and took the flask. She wasn't used to drinking gin with a mixer, never mind straight. The first swallow seared the back of her throat. But the second went down more smoothly and the third was perfectly pleasant. Within minutes she could feel the liquor in her extremities—tingling at the tips of her fingers and toes. Then like tendrils of ivy, it began climbing her arms and legs, presumably en route to her head.

Eve rolled down the window and closed her eyes as the in-rushing air tore at the pages of her pad. Following suit, Olivia opened her window and leaned into the breeze along Sunset as the brightly lit marquees leaned back—boasting of World Premieres and Held Over by Popular Demands.

It was true what Eve had said: Olivia had been busy.

How many roles had she played since she had come to Hollywood? Fourteen? Fifteen? She had lost count. First, there was Dolly Stevens; then the guileless Lucille and innocent Hermia. Arabella, Angela, Elsa, and Cath. Maria, Germain, and Serena. Each one as demure as the last.

—So, of all the men in Los Angeles to dine with, why

the Big White Hat?

Olivia looked back from the window to find Eve holding out the flask. Olivia took another drink.

—It was arranged.

—*Arranged*? What are you, Amish?

Olivia laughed.

—Arranged by the studio.

—Do they normally tell you who to dine with?

—Oh, they'll tell me who to dine with, all right. They'll pick the restaurant. The table. They practically pick my entrée.

Eve looked a little surprised.

—I'm on contract, Olivia explained. When you're on contract the studio doesn't just decide what roles you take; it weighs in on whatever might affect your public image: what you wear, how you spend your weekends, who you spend them with . . .

Eve whistled.

—You should have the world on a string, sister.

—It's the other way around, I'm afraid.

A perfect example sprang to mind, and Olivia almost launched into its petty details. But she regretted having allowed herself to go on at such length already. What a prima donna she must have sounded like. Complaining about the life of a Hollywood star. So she shook her head and said nothing.

But Eve had been watching her closely.

—Speak now, she warned, or forever hold your peace.

Olivia met her gaze.

—All right, she said after a moment. Have you read *Gone with the Wind*?

—I'm not much of a reader.

—Well, it's a bestseller and they're making it into a movie at Selznick. The main character is a spoiled, tempestuous figure—and it seems like every actress in Hollywood is vying to play her except for me. But the second lead, she's a counterweight to Scarlett. She's more upright and sweet, yet every bit as strong. At any rate, the director thinks I'm perfect for the part; and I think he may be right.

—Sounds great.

—But you see, it's a violation of my contract to even *talk* with Cukor. He's gone so far as to suggest that I read for the part covertly. He wants me to put on a scarf and tinted glasses and come up the back drive of his house on a Sunday afternoon—like a thief, or a spy.

—Even better! said Eve.

Olivia laughed, but shook her head.

—Jack Warner, my studio chief, would never let me be in that film. He's said as much already. I think he's furious he's not making the movie himself. But you have to understand that this sort of thing goes part and parcel with the rest of it. And it's not like I'll be sitting on my hands. They have me slotted for two other parts at Warner this spring.

As Olivia spoke, she could tell that Eve felt a sense of disappointment. Perhaps to mask it, Eve took a drink from the flask and then turned to the window where the marquees had given way to the grand eucalyptus trees at the edge of the Brentwood cul de sacs. When Eve turned back she said simply:

—Don't be your own worst enemy, Livvy.

Olivia nodded and looked out her own window.

—It's been a long time since someone called me Livvy, she said.

STRETCHING A HUNDRED YARDS into the sea, the Santa Monica piers were crowded with all manner of amusements. There were tin rifle ranges where brand-new recruits in freshly pressed uniforms tested their aim and rainbow-colored wheels of fortune ten feet in diameter surrounded by Mexican grandmothers who crossed themselves at every spin. Polishing off their flask of gin, and ditching their shoes in the sand, Eve and Olivia wandered forth into the carnival, beckoned by the calls of barkers and the rumble of roller coasters and the shouts of children out past their bedtimes.

It didn't take long for them to find the fabled purveyor of donuts—standing proudly under a green-and-white canopy. While Eve paid for their order, Olivia watched the freshly fried donuts riding the small conveyor until they dropped into the sugar pan, one by one—and she was suddenly struck by how hungry she was. It was the hunger of a lifetime of half-finished dinners and prematurely tamped out cigarettes. So, when Eve pulled the first of the donuts from the bag, Olivia grabbed it and took a wolfish bite.

And what a donut it was! A confection of contrasts, of contradictions. First, came the exterior—hot, crusty, coated with a grit of sugar. But then this golden brown sensation was followed almost impossibly by the cool smoothness of the jelly. You could tell it wasn't raspberry or strawberry. And that was the genius of it. It was simply sweet and red. A finer preserve would have ruined the whole sensation.

When Olivia took her second bite, she could feel a glob of the jelly running down her chin.

—That, said Eve, is the first real smile that I've seen on you all night.

As the two of them continued down the pier, the autumn wind seemed to be gaining force, pulling carnations from lapels and ribbons from pigtails. Grabbing Eve's elbow, Olivia pointed as a fine yellow hat blew off the head of a Negress. Her boyfriend gave honorable chase; but when the hat lofted out to sea, he took off his own hat and spun it like a discus into the dark.

—The wind, said Eve. It's incredible.

—The Santa Ana. It comes every autumn.

—From *where*?

—From all the talk.

Eve laughed.

—You mean from the gossip?

—And the auditions and directions and negotiations . . .

From the heart-crossed promises, thought Olivia, and the heartfelt excuses. All those voices rising from Burbank and Beverly Hills like a tide until they breeched some invisible barrier and flooded toward the sea, threatening to tear up the palm trees and personas and plot twists in their wake.

Now it was Eve who reached for Olivia's elbow.

A few steps away was an elaborate contraption: a machine that looked like a cross between a fire engine and a calliope and half the technological advances of the twentieth century. It had pistons like you'd see on a locomotive, the dials and meters of a furnace, an elaborate system of eggbeaters. There were multicolored pinwheels and whistles and the horn of a gramophone mounted on a pole.

Standing before it was a little man with the beard and pince nez of Toulouse-Lautrec.

Eve popped the last bite of donut into her mouth and wiped the sugar from her hands.

—So what's this all about?

—This? the man repeated. Why, this is the Astrologicon.

The three of them surveyed it together.

—You will note, the little man continued, that I said *the* instead of *an*. For, it is the only one of its kind.

He explained this somewhat sadly, as if he were speaking of the very last of some fantastic species like the unicorn or chimera.

—But what does it do? asked Olivia.

—Ah . . . , he said. What does it do.

With two fingers and a thumb, he sharpened the point of his beard.

—Once in possession of five essential attributes of a Homo sapiens, the Astrologicon will consult the laws of chemistry and the arrangement of the stars in order to provide an unassailable, incontrovertible, and indismissible instruction. For one dollar.

—Let's to it, said Eve.

The proprietor accepted Eve's payment and placed it with ceremony in a small tin box. Then he proceeded to collect the essential attributes of her person and to calibrate the contraption accordingly. He punched the letters of her name into a panel of dislodged typewriter keys. He set three adjacent dials to the year, month, and date of her birth. He took a fingerprint. He turned an arrow embedded in a spectrum of colors to the precise pigmentation of her eyes. And finally, he handed Eve the end of a stethoscope that was cabled back into the inner workings of the machine.

—If you would be so kind, he said, pointing shyly toward her sternum.

Eve slid the stethoscope under the neckline of her dress and you could suddenly hear the beating of her heart broadcast through the gramophone's horn. As Eve and Olivia realized what they were hearing, the tempo of Eve's heartbeat increased. But closing her eyes, Eve exhaled and inhaled and exhaled again, until her heartbeat subsided to the tempo of the waves beneath the pier.

The proprietor nodded in sober appreciation. Then after reclaiming the stethoscope, he reached into his watch pocket and produced a hexagon of brass.

—I caution you, young lady, that the Astrologicon is not to be taken lightly. I suspect the path of your life appears clearly before you—a path that in all probability is popular, convenient, and profitable. But the Astrologicon cares nothing for popularity, convenience, or profit. Rather, like the Oracle at Delphi it will advise you to do what you should regardless of opinion, difficulty, and cost.

He handed the hexagon to Eve and gestured to a slot in the machine marked by four converging arrows. Then he put his hands together and bowed.

Without a moment's hesitation, Eve dropped the token in the slot.

There was a buzz followed by a whir. The needles on the temperature gauges began to climb and after a blast of steam the axles of the engine set in motion the pistons and pinwheels. The proprietor led them down the length of the machine, pointing to each kinetic phase—to the interpolator and the centrifuge and the epistemolog—until with the ring of a desk clerk's bell, an envelope fell into a sterling silver toast caddy.

The envelope was addressed in fine calligraphy to *Evelyn Ross—November 5th, 1938*. Eve thanked the proprietor. Then she led Olivia to an uncrowded spot under a lamppost and placed the envelope in her hand.

—Livvy, whatever this says—I think you should follow it to the letter.

Olivia didn't smile at the suggestion. She only nodded and closed her fingers around the envelope.

Then the two continued their progress past the roller coaster toward the very end of the pier where they could now see the ocean-going casinos bobbing outside the city limits. And it felt to Olivia as if the continent was being tilted and all of California was going to slip into the sea. And though she couldn't remember the exact reference—and whether it was from mythology or the Bible—she knew instinctively as they approached the pier's limit that she mustn't look back.

LITSKY

THE GIRLS ON THE dance floor at El Rey's came in all his favorite colors. There were girls from across the Rio Grande with tequila-colored skin who liked to wag their fingers and shake their heads in coy dissuasion. There were girls from Alabama and New Orleans who had skin the color of bourbon and dispositions twice as sweet. And the girls from the islands came as black as a glass of rum molasses. Ochre, tawny, bronze, beaver, russet, pistol, pitch: Litsky had a taste for them all. So what did he care, if he was the only cracker on Shepherd Avenue. What did he care, if he was the only cracker in all of L.A.

BACK IN THE AVENUE's holy-rolling heyday, the Laurel Canyon limousines would idle at the curb from Friday night until the Sunday sermons. It was a colored town to be sure, but one with painted porches and barbershop poles. Bernie the Weisenheimer (who had a nose for making money off of those who couldn't make it off of themselves), he bought a roadhouse on an empty block and christened it the Rum Tum Club. He slapped tuxedos on the boys in the band and dropped some red leather booths around the four-tops. Then he ran a rope right down the middle of the dance floor, so the ises and aints would know where to do their dancing.

But after the Crash, Bernie went bust right along with the neighborhood. The porch paint peeled, the candy stripes stalled, and the highfalutins headed for higher ground. By the summer of '36, when a Harlemite by way of Havana reopened the club as El Rey's, he didn't need a rope to keep the order on the dance floor anymore; but he left it lying there just the same. And as the bands played a jazz as half-bred as he was, the local girls would sweat through their dresses and shimmy over that rope with relish.

That's why Litsky couldn't believe his eyes when the front door opened at eleven p.m. and in walked Miss Olivia de Havilland in a strappy red dress. She was on the arm of that ravaged blonde he'd heard about, the one who'd come out of nowhere. With the blonde leading the way, the girls took one of the tables near the band and ordered tequilas and lime as if they'd been born in the barrio.

EARLIER THAT YEAR, Litsky had followed Dehavvy around a bit like everybody else—but what a waste of shoe leather. The boys at the studio had her on a short leash and it showed. She was all seltzer at six, supper at seven, and safely home by nine for some Mother Goose and milk before they tightly tucked her in. But then, you really couldn't blame them. They knew exactly what they were sitting on: the 79th element.

Because on every Saturday night in every small town in America—after milking the pigs and slopping the cows—Fred and Edna were headed for the picture show. And while in exchange for their hard-earned nickels they surely hoped to see an escapade, once they'd traveled all that way to merry old England, it was the girl next door who they hoped to find on the throne.

And Dehavvy was just the ticket. As genteely in person as she was on the screen.

Yes, Siree Bob. When Fred and Edna sat at their kitchen table with their pickup cooling in the yard, as they were savoring their happily-ever-after over one last piece of pie, they could feel as proud of Dehavvy as if they'd raised her.

Knowing everything there was to know about getting his money's worth, Jack Warner had been working Dehavvy like a horse—strapping her to a new picture every three or four months. And now the word on Wilshire was that old Jack was set to lend her out for a part in *Gone with the Wind*, thanks to a big fat IOU with Selznick's name on it and a little arm-twisting by Mrs. Warner herself on Dehavvy's behalf.

So this blonde from nowhere must have had the boys at the studios tearing their hair out. From across the room you could see that no one had a leash on her. While Dehavvy looked like she'd never seen a dance floor, the blonde was taking things in with the narrowed eyes of a killer. She was sussing up the place and she liked what she saw. She liked the band, the tempo, the tequila—the whole shebang. If Dehavvy was bandying about with the likes of this one, then you wouldn't have long to wait for the wrong place and the wrong time to have their tearful reunion.

UNBEKNOWNST TO THE SPICE OF LIFE, the band began playing their trumpety little number for the third time. Some sort of cross between a mariachi and a rumba, this song would skip along for twenty measures and then all the boys in the band would stop on a beat and shout *La Casa!* before picking up where they'd left off. When they played the number for the second time, Litsky rolled his eyes with everyone else—thinking, *amateurs*. But when they struck it up for the third time, the crowd broke into a head-shaking grin. Maybe the gauchos were a little more soused, or maybe they were itching to showcase the steps they'd practiced in take two, because before you knew it, they had dragged their dates back on the floor and grabbed them by the hips.

Dehavvy would have been blushing, if she weren't so busy blinking. All of twenty-two, weighing in at a hundred and one pounds with shoulder blades poking through her skin, she looked better than she had in '37—but she was still a year's worth of good living away from looking like a woman.

—Hey. Shorty.

Litsky looked back from the dance floor.

It was the lazy baritone behind the bar. He was drying his hands with a dirty rag.

—You gonna have a drink? Or you gonna sit there all night?

—What's your hurry?

—That perch is for the parched.

—Yeah, yeah . . .

Litsky took a bill from his pocket and tossed it on the bar.

—Gimme a Scotch on the rocks. And this time, pour it from a bottle instead of a jar.

Ol' Man River shuffled off and came back with the drink and the change. Litsky left a nickel on the counter to show his heartfelt appreciation for the five-star service. Then he turned on his stool, leaned his back against the bar, and stirred his whiskey with a finger.

At the table by the band, the blonde was nodding her

head to the beat of the claves with a that's-more-like-it sort of smile. She took a drag from a cigarette and shot a column of smoke at the ceiling.

McNulty, that knucklehead, had heard from someone who'd heard from someone that she was a moll on the run from Chicago. Besides the fact that molls on the run don't hide out in Hollywood, the caption didn't jive with the candid. There was definitely a streak of the privileged class in this one. Becker, the two-bit stringer, claimed she was another Kraut flown in by von Sternberg. But that didn't figure either. This blonde had a joi de vivre that couldn't get a visa to the Rhineland.

She was leaning forward now to say something to Dehavvy. She pointed at the percussionist with a discerning cigarette. Dehavvy listened and nodded with the rapt attention of the newly under wing.

Who the hell is she? Litsky found himself thinking, for once.

And he would have let his mind dwell on that quandary, if down the bar two Tijuana roosters hadn't begun disturbing the peace. Que es eso? the one on his feet was saying for the second time. The seated one turned on his stool like a spokesman for ten generations of family feuding. When he stood on principle, he knocked over his barstool. Ol' Man River drifted upstream. He put his big black hands on the bar and told them to take it outside; but he didn't need to. The first one spat on the floor and headed for the exit with two of his kin. The other one counted to ten, then signaled his amigos who were picking their teeth at a table nearby.

Spics.

Litsky shook his head and shifted his gaze back to the business at hand. While the blonde studied the band, Dehavvy peeked over her straw like a schoolgirl. Like a cousin from out of town. Like the ward of the king of England.

Litsky took a good, long look at Dehavvy, then back at the second pack of Tijuanans who were swaggering out the door in the footsteps of the first. Then he took his nickel back off the bar. He went to the phone near the boys' room and dialed the 77th Street precinct.

—I'd like to report a knife fight, he said into the receiver—Yeah, that's right, a knife fight—In the parking lot of El Rey's—On Shepherd off Central—When'd it happen? Any minute now.

Litsky hung up.

This is going to be interesting, he thought to himself like a philosopher.

But when he returned to his stool, Dehavvy and the blonde were gone.

Shit.

Litsky studied the path from their table to the little girls' room; then, short on hope, he scanned the club from end to end. But lo and behold, there they were: Elbow-to-elbow on the dance floor.

The band was playing a Mexicali *Begin the Beguine*. Either by order of the front man, or through some collective instinct, all the boys had gotten on one side of the rope and the girls had gotten on the other. The band's take on the number had some advanced mathematics and the local girls were making the most of it. They were doing long division with their hips and shaking their cans to the thirteenth power. Dehavvy and the blonde couldn't keep up. They didn't have the bodies for it, or the backgrounds. But they were indisputably in the mix.

Maybe you had to give the blonde credit for taking Dehavvy to El Rey's, after all. Because if anyone on the dance floor knew who she was, they weren't showing it. By the time the locals got to El Rey's, they'd had their fill of deference for the day. (Yes, ma'am. No, ma'am. Thank you, ma'am.) And with their eyes half closed, swaying like a crowd of cocoanut trees, they were plenty primed for some rapture serene.

At least, that's what Litsky was thinking when the band broke into *Mi Casa* for the fourth time. Within a beat, every seat in the house was empty. The blonde and Dehavvy had taken places on opposite sides of the rope now and were matching each other step-for-step—shaking their heads in tandem and waiting for the twentieth measure, when they could stand on their toes and shout *Mi Casa!* with the rest of them.

Despite the clamor, Litsky could hear the sweet, unmistakable sound of sirens in the distance. He looked back toward the club's entrance in time to see a tall, thin kid in chauffeur's getup come scrambling through the door. He took off his hat like he was entering a church. When his eyes lit on the blonde, he made a beeline for the dance floor.

Litsky got off his stool.

The kid beckoned her to the edge of the floor and whispered in her ear. From across the room Litsky could see her eyes narrow; then she rattled off instructions like a drill sergeant; and as the kid headed back to his car, she grabbed Dehavvy by the hand. She led her through the crowd, behind the bandstand, and toward the kitchen door.

Litsky snatched his bag from under his stool. He hoisted himself onto the bar and swung his legs over it, toppling a bottle of beer.

—Hey! Ol' Man River shouted from around the bend.

Litsky scurried out the loading door into the night.

Rounding the back of the club, he could see the lights of the kitch-en shining through the screen door just as a pine green Packard appeared from the other direction. Litsky was barely ready when the door swung open and out came the blonde dragging Dehavvy behind her. Litsky steadied himself, whistled, and pulled the trig-ger. With a great pop the flash went off. Sparks fell to the ground filling the air with the smell of brimstone. The blonde wouldn't let go of Dehavvy until she had her safely in the car; then with her teeth bared, she turned toward Litsky—but he was gone.

He was already cutting a wide circle through the un-derbrush headed toward Central Ave, where he'd had the good sense to leave his car. He slipped under the wheel, set her in gear, and turned onto Shepherd. In the lot of El Rey's he could see the cops conferring in a tight circumference with los Capuletos y los Montagues. He saluted them all as he passed, and then he switched on the radio.

It was another heart warmer from that happy-go-lucky huckster, Bing Crosby

He hated Bing Crosby.

But he left the dial where it was and found himself sing-ing along. For in the instant the flash had gone off and the girls had looked up in surprise, as clear as crystal he could see that De-havvy had stepped on the hem of her dress while scampering out the door. Because her left shoulder strap had snapped free—and peeking out from behind the silky red fabric was a million-dollar indiscretion.

As Litsky drove along Santa Monica Blvd., he watched the buildings slinking past his windshield. It was like turning the

pages of the *Oxford History of Class Acts*: At the corner of High-land Ave was the hotel where Errol Flynn had tried to lower himself from a third floor window by a towel; two doors down from La Brea was the Cancan where Gloria Swanson had almost plucked out the eyes of the Blue Angel; and a few blocks later, he passed Antonio's, where Louis Mayer had begun dining on lettuce for fear that he soon wouldn't be able to cross his fat little fingers when crossing his heart and hoping to die.

On the sixth floor of the Fulwilder building the lights were out in the corner office, which figured. Humpty Dumpty must have waddled back to his bungalow in order to catch up on the sleep he hadn't got behind his desk all day.

Litsky turned onto Fairfax and pulled into O'Malley's. As usual, the place was empty. O'Malley himself was standing on a pantry stool taking down the colored lights that were still hanging behind the bar.

—Hey, Santy Claus.

O'Malley looked back with a grimace. He stepped off the stool, leaving the lights swinging from a hook.

—A round on me for everyone in the house, said Litsky.

—Hardy har, said O'Malley.

He grabbed a bottle by the neck like it was a duck he was about to strangle. Once he'd poured the whiskey, he finally took in Litsky's expression.

—You look like the canary in the coal mine, he observed.

—It's the cat who caught the canary, you flummox. But you're on the right track.

—Cats, coal mines, said O'Malley with a shrug. What gives?

Litsky waggled his empty glass and put it on the bar.

—Just keep these coming. Then maybe I'll teach you a

thing or two about this town.

O'Malley reached for the bottle and Litsky headed for the phone booth in back. After shutting himself in, he took off his hat and pulled a scrap of paper from the inside band. Ragged and stained it was scratched with five different numbers that were none too easy to come by. Litsky dialed the fifth. Even from the sleepy style in which he drawled *Hello*, you could tell that Marcus Benton was an educated man. A measured man. A man who knew the difference between the pennywise and the poundfoolish.

—This is Jeremiah Litsky, Litsky said into the receiver—That's right, that Litsky—Yeah, I know what time it is—Never mind how I got your number. You'll be glad I've got it—That's it, counselor. I've a certain something you'll want to get your hands on—How big? You're going to need a ladder to see over it—You know the diner on Wilshire & Clay?—Maybe you should come see me there some time. Like tomorrow at eight. And bring your wallet.

Litsky rang off.

Because here's the thing: Fred and Edna loved to see the girl next door, all right—sitting on the tippity top of the silvery screen. But the only thing they loved more than that was seeing her tumble back down. That didn't mean Fred and Edna were bad people. There wasn't a mean-spirited bone in their bodies. They just couldn't help themselves. The scientists call it human nature; which is just a fancy term for the God-given flaws we have no intention of giving back.

Litsky put the scrap in his hat and his hat on his head. Then he put another nickel in the phone. He didn't need to look up this number. He knew every crummy digit by heart. After sixteen rings, Humpty got around to hefting the receiver.

—It's me, Litsky—Yeah, I know what time it is. Everybody knows what time it is—What's so important? I quit, that's what—Wait a second. Can you say that slower? So I can write it down? It's one for the history books—Yeah. Same to you.

Litsky hung up and exited the booth. When he got back to his stool, his drink was waiting for him.

And so was the ravaged blonde.

She was sitting alone at the opposite end of the bar.

He couldn't believe it. She must have seen him saluting the boys from Shepherd Avenue and ordered the kid to follow in hot pursuit. And now here she was, giving him the nod of a solid citizen who's just happened to happen into a bar.

When she ordered a Scotch and soda, Litsky told O'Malley to put it on his tab. She gave a neighborly smile of thanks, then she walked her drink down the bar.

—Hi, she said. I'm Katey. Katey Kontent.

—Jeremiah Litsky.

She gestured to a table for two in the middle of the room.

—Would you like to join me, Mr. Litsky?

—Sure, said Mr. Litsky.

As he was reaching for his bag, she picked up his drink and carried it to the table on his behalf. It was only when they'd both taken their seats that he could see what a knockout she'd been. All blonde and blue with a spunky little hourglass figure to boot. She wasn't Litsky's type, but without the scar and the limp she would have been everybody else's.

Tough break, he thought to himself, feeling a tremor of something that might have been mistaken for sympathy.

She raised her glass and they drank without taking their eyes off each other.

Or maybe he had it all wrong . . .

Maybe in this town the scar was just the ticket. In Hollywood, when a good looker gets off the bus, every dame for twenty miles grits her teeth. And when the boys in the business meet a pretty face, they've got good reason to be wary—because they'll never really know what she's after until she's after it. But with that scar, there weren't going to be any screen tests for the likes of Katey Kontent.

Which made you sort of wonder what she was doing here in the first place.

As Litsky was thinking this through, she was sitting with her legs crossed, sipping at her drink and flipping her shoe off her heel—letting it hang on the tip of her toe for a beat before flipping it back on.

—So what do you do, Mr. Litsky?

He stirred his Scotch with a finger.

—I'm a member of the fourth estate.

—A journalist? she said taking out a cigarette. Well, that must be fascinating in a town like this. Tell me all about it.

She sat there with the unlit cigarette between her fingers waiting for Litsky to strike a match. He took a drink of his whiskey instead.

—You can cut the sugar, Blondie. I know exactly who you are.

—And who pray tell is that?

—You're the one who comes in through the lobby and goes out through the kitchen door.

Pleased by his own poetry, Litsky smiled for the first time in a year.

—Ooh, she replied. What big teeth you have, Grandma.

Litsky raised his glass in the affirmative and emptied it in her honor.

—You want to know what this town is like? he said. I'll

tell you what it's like. It's like a waiting room. It's the largest waiting room in the world. We're all sitting on wooden benches reading yesterday's papers, eating yesterday's lunch. But every now and then, the door to the platform opens and the conductor lets one of us through for a ride on the Millionaire Express. Sometimes, it's some kid in a mailroom whose story's found its way to a big oak desk. Sometimes, it's a dainty damsel like your friend who gets plucked off the farm. But sometimes, it's for a little guy like me.

He patted the bag that was sitting on the table.

—And when that door opens . . . , he added.

—You'd better go through it, because it may not open again.

—Bingo, Blondie.

She put her chin on her hand and looked at him all dreamy.

—That's a nice little mustache you've got there, Mr. Litsky. How do you do that? How do you leave just that little bit behind?

—I've got a light touch.

—I'll bet you have. Now I've got a story for you, she said—finally taking the time to light her own cigarette, shaking the flame from the match and tossing it over her shoulder.

The story was about a fat, little Italian who happened to make it good. This guinea designed scenery for the opera houses in Milan and New York before making his way out west. Well, once he'd poked his finger through a Hollywood set, he sent for all the boys back home—you know, the carpenters and painters and masons who'd built the Sistine Chapel, but who were fresh off the boat and willing to ply their trades for a nickel a day. Pretty soon, all the studios wanted to hire this guy. He's building Dodge Cities, and African jungles, and rooms in Versailles, making half a million bucks a year. So, naturally, he tears down his little shack on Doheny and has his boys build him a mansion with all the fixings. He moves back in on August first, 1935, and the following morning, they find him floating in his pool.

Litsky well remembered the heat wave of '35. In fact, as he was sitting in O'Malley's listening to this yarn, he could practically feel the swelter; he could practically hear the water lapping at the edge of the pool as the cruisers pulled into the drive.

Quick as a wink, the cops see that this was no ordinary accident. There was no bump on his head, no booze in his blood. So they start wondering: Did one of those vendettas get carried over from the old country? Did one of his *paisanos* finally get tired of working for nickels? Or, was the competition getting antsy?

Blondie leaned back and shot some smoke at the ceiling.

—But in the end, Mr. Litsky, do you know what it was that killed him?

—No, said Litsky, wiping his brow. What?

—The metric system.

Litsky shook his head.

—The metric system . . . ?

—You see, our little entrepreneur didn't know how to swim. So when the pool was being built, he told his mason to make it a yard and a half deep—that way, he could wade in it safely with his head above water. But the mason, having just arrived in America, didn't know what a yard was. And when he asked, one of his countrymen told him it was just like a meter. But, as you know Mr. Litsky, a meter is a little longer than a yard. So that's what this man's ticket on the Millionaire Express bought him: Five extra inches of water.

Litsky stood to go. But the room moved a little to the left.

—That's a helluva story, Blondie.

He reached for his bag. He knew there was something important in it. Something like his future. Or maybe it was his past. He couldn't remember. But either way, it was heavy as hell.

—Here, said a motherly voice. Let me help you with that.

Freed of its burden, Litsky's body floated a foot off the ground. It hovered for a second, and then settled back in its chair.

On the shelf behind the bar a tiny orchestra was playing that trumpety little number for the seventeenth time. Litsky put a hand on the table and tried to stand again, but he couldn't budge. He shook the inner workings of his head, and for a moment he could clearly see the features of this blonde who'd come out of nowhere. She was studying him the way that she had studied the band—with her narrowed eyes and her that's-more-like-it sort of smile.

She leaned over him so closely, he could smell her perfume.

—Where did you come from? he heard himself asking.

—From a hurricane, she said.

Then the warm circumference of her beauty began to recede, diffuse, and finally disappear.

On the periphery of his awareness, someone a lot like Litsky knocked over a chair. Its clatter echoed through the hallowed halls of Hollywood, mimicking the geometric pattern of the tin ceiling overhead. A door closed, an orchestra abandoned its search for the twentieth measure, and a string of gently swinging Christmas lights went out one by one, leaving Litsky in the ebon embrace of the eternities.

MARCUS

ON THE FIRST OF MARCH, Marcus Benton parted the louvers of his window shade with two fingers and looked out onto the lot, thinking he still wasn't used to the weather. Without a bleak winter hour or sweltering summer night, February hadn't felt like February anymore than July would feel like July. In Southern California, it was as if a glimpse of spring were repeated week after week, month after month, year after year.

Central Casting must have been listening to his thoughts, because a barefooted boy wearing a floppy straw hat suddenly appeared from around Building Four with a makeshift rod on his shoulder.

As a boy, Marcus could have assembled a better one with his eyes closed. He could have stripped a sapling, bent and threaded a needle, tied a double hinge. Having slipped out the back of the schoolhouse, he could have skirted the town hall to avoid the feed store and circled back to Keeper's Hollow, where Whistling Billy McGuire would have already dropped his line. But here in Culver City, the boy with the floppy hat was stopped by a young blonde in a bright blue blouse. She asked him a question and he pointed toward Marcus's office.

Marcus let the louvers fall.

He resumed his place behind his desk and took up the small green dossier. A glance at the photograph inside confirmed that the blonde in blue was the one he was waiting for. He leafed through the file, reacquainting himself with what little they knew: that she had been raised in New York, attended a finishing school in Europe, worked for a year at a literary press; and that she had fled the gossip mill of Manhattan when her engagement to a blue-blooded banker had been abruptly called off.

He wished, of course, that he knew more (one always did). But what he had in hand would suffice. For it was a simple matter, really—a matter of making the young woman feel a part of a grander endeavor.

Marcus had learned this in his early days as a litigator in Arkansas. In the jury box of the Pulaski County Courthouse (in any jury box in the country, for that matter), one could expect to find a sample of the human condition: a patchwork of intellects and experiences, personalities and prejudices. To convince these twelve disparate souls of an argument's merits, an attorney could not rely on logic, or science, or even justice. After all, Socrates couldn't convince the elders of Athens of his innocence, anymore than Galileo could convince the pope, or Jesus Christ the people of Jerusalem. To convince the men of a jury, one must instead draw them into the course of events.

One must show that they have not been called to the courthouse to fulfill some civic obligation—to observe and assess. Rather, they have been called to participate. Each juror is a principal who must play his part in the trial as one plays his part at a family gathering, or at the supper table of a friend, or in the pew of a church—those places where consciously or unconsciously we know the frailties and strengths of our neighbors to be inseparable from our own.

That is how Marcus extricated David from his little problem back in Arkansas. Thanks to the papers, weeks before the trial the good people of Little Rock already knew that Selznick was a Hollywood mogul. They knew he was a millionaire, a city slicker, a Jew. And this was the essence of opposing counsel's case. Thus, acknowledging that all of this was true, Marcus (his suit a little rumpled, his hair a little unkempt) took the jury back to the beginning. Calling David to the stand, Marcus inquired about his youth in a blue-collar corner of Pittsburgh; he inquired how David at the age of twenty-one had helped his family make ends meet when his father fell on hard times; overcoming objections of relevancy, Marcus inquired how David had fallen in love with the cinema at the age of ten—tucked among his fellow citizens in a crowded theater, thrilling to the sound of the upright piano and the flicker of celluloid, imagining a day when the Lone Ranger would call Hi ho, Silver aloud . . .

Six months later, Marcus found himself pursuing a similar line of questioning in Los Angeles County Court.

When David had called, Marcus demurred. But David had been characteristically persuasive: It would only take a few weeks, he said; he would make it worth Marcus's while; and there was no one else in the whole country he could rely upon. As an added enticement, David sent a plane. With Marcus seated by himself in the passenger cabin (a glass of his favorite bourbon in hand), the plane inscribed its dotted line from Little Rock across the dustbowl, over the Grand Canyon and Death Valley, to the airstrip in Culver City where David waited at the side of his Rolls Royce. And when they arrived at Selznick International and walked into Building Two, David opened an oaken door with an elaborate flourish to reveal . . . Marcus's office in Little Rock.

With a bit of help from the property department, the Selznick International set designers had engineered a facsimile—right down to the louvered shades, the antiquated map of eastern Arkansas, and the Roman bust on the book shelf (albeit a papier-mâché Caesar standing in for a marble Cicero.)

That was four years ago.

Marcus surveyed the top of his desk. Neatly arranged along its edge were seven stacks of paper, one of which stood a foot tall. *These* weren't from the prop department. They were an essential component of the industriousness of his client—a man for whom no slight was too offhand, no promise too in passing, no penny too thin to wage a legal battle on its behalf. Selznick versus a Studio. Selznick versus a Star. Selznick v. Temperature, Time, and Tide.

—Mr. Benton, sounded an electronic voice. A Miss Evelyn Ross here to see you.

Marcus put the dossier in the drawer and pushed the button on the intercom.

—Please, show her in.

As was his habit, Marcus came around the desk ready to greet his guest and make her feel at ease; but he was taken aback when through the door came the blonde in blue with the bare-footed boy's fishing rod on her shoulder and his floppy straw hat on her head.

She barely gave him a chance to introduce himself.

—Did you know that a few hundred yards from here is a stretch of the Mississippi River? And not only does it have a rickety dock and a riverboat, it has been stocked with actual fish!

Marcus laughed.

—We do strive for verisimilitude, Miss Ross.

—I'll remember that.

She gestured with the rod toward the bookcase.

—May I?

—Of course.

She leaned the rod upright and placed the hat on the shelf next to Caesar's head. Then she took a seat, crossed her legs, and lightly bounced her foot.

Inwardly, Marcus smiled. Because in the course of sixty seconds, he had learned more about Evelyn Ross than the studio's investigators had learned in three weeks. The young lady sitting before him was no native of New York. The ease of manner, the disarming smile, the glimmer in the eye were all indigenous to that tribe of women who dwell from the shores of the Great Lakes to the port of New Orleans. Over the course of two hundred years, these farm-bred charms had evolved to provide the rest of us some consolation when losing the upper hand in horse-trading, card-play, and courtship.

If an engagement had been broken back in New York, Marcus thought to himself, then Evelyn Ross was the one who had done the breaking.

She pointed to the seven stacks of paper.

—Do you buy that stuff by the pound?

—You jest, Miss Ross. But my father ran a feed store in Arkansas. I spent my summers selling all manner of things by the pound; not to mention by the bushel and the peck.

—That must have made you quite hardy.

—It made me very good at estimating weights.

—Really, she said with a playful squint. Then how heavy am I?

—That's not the sort of question a gentleman should answer.

—I'm not the type to take offense.

He tilted his head.

—105 pounds . . . ?

—Not bad! You're only off by two.

—Was I heavy or light?

—Now, *that's* going a step too far.

Oh, Marcus could see why a young banker in Manhattan might have made a rushed proposal; and he could see why it wouldn't stick. He even felt a touch of pity for the poor bastard. But it did make one wonder: If the young man was the jilted party, then why had Miss Ross left New York?

She swung her foot up and down, waiting for him to speak.

—I appreciate your coming on such short notice, he began. I hope it wasn't too much of an inconvenience.

—Not at all.

—I'm glad to hear it. The reason we asked you to stop by is very straightforward. In essence, we want to thank you. We know that you and Miss de Havilland have become good friends; but it has also been brought to our attention that back in January you helped her out of quite a fix . . .

—What are friends for, she said.

—Precisely, Miss Ross. What are friends for. Miss de Havilland is a wonderful young woman with a bright future. But as you've seen firsthand, there are those who would seek to profit from her slightest misstep. So, we would deem it a terrific favor if you would continue to keep an eye out for her.

—Who is this *we* you keep mentioning, Mr. Benton? Is there someone hiding back there—behind all those stacks of paper?

—No, Marcus said with a smile. By *we*, I generally refer to the studio. But more specifically, I'm referring to Mr. Selznick, our chief; and Jack Warner over at Warner Brothers, where Miss de Havilland is still under contract. They both have a keen interest in Miss de Havilland's welfare.

—Ah, said Miss Ross. And exactly what sorts of missteps are they imagining? Surely they're not afraid of another broken shoulder strap?

—Of course not, said Marcus with a light laugh (followed by a thoughtful pause). Through no fault of her own, a young woman in Miss de Havilland's position is exposed to a variety of hazards. Over the course of time, there are bound to be . . . unfortunate encounters . . . awkward entanglements . . . ill-advised alliances . . .

Miss Ross exhibited an expression of mild surprise.

—Encounters, entanglements, and alliances! Mr. Benton, keeping an eye on all that doesn't sound like a favor. It sounds like a job . . .

Having let their minds wander in the heat of the afternoon, the disparate souls of the jury looked up in unison. For whether they had spent their years of Christian toil on the floor of a mill or behind a plow—a day's wage for a day's work was something they well understood.

Mr. Benton opened his mouth.

Miss Ross raised her eyebrows.

But it was an impatient voice in the waiting room that broke the silence.

They both looked back at the replicated oaken door, which flew open to admit a man in his late thirties with rolled up sleeves and wire-rimmed glasses.

—Is this her?

—David . . .

He turned to look at Miss Ross.

—What does she say?

—We were just finishing up. I'll come and find you on the set as soon as we're done.

Ignoring Marcus, David pushed back the stacks of paper and sat on the edge of the desk.

—Miss Ross, isn't it? I'm David O. Selznick, the head of the studio.

David paused to make sure the full measure of this declaration could be taken. When Miss Ross acted suitably impressed, he continued:

—At this moment, we are in the midst of making what could well be the greatest motion picture of all time. And I have left the set for one reason: to tell you the most closely guarded secret of Hollywood.

Miss Ross cast a quick glance at Marcus, then sat up with an expression of scholastic enthusiasm. While for his part, David barreled ahead—speaking with his trademark urgency, attention to detail, and utter disregard for whether what he was saying was furthering or confounding his purpose.

—Without a doubt, there are Titanic personalities at the helm of Hollywood. And to those who read the papers, it must seem that we alone deserve the credit or condemnation for what reaches the screen. But making a movie is a *contingent* art, Miss Ross. Yes, a great producer starts with a vision and personally assembles its elements. After an extensive search, he chooses the Mona Lisa as his model. He selects a dress that will drape across her shoulders just so. He arranges her hair. He locates the perfect landscape as a backdrop. He makes her comfortable, unself-conscious. Then patiently, he waits for her to express her innermost humanity through a smile so that he can capture it on canvas. But at that very moment, the studio doors fling open to admit an onslaught of actors and extras, stuntmen and cameramen, foley artists, fitters, gaffers, best boys—every one of whom brandishes a brush.

David spoke of his employees with a grimace, as if their arrival signaled civilization's second descent into the Dark Ages.

—What I am telling you, Miss Ross, is that every single one of the two hundred men and women I have enlisted to help make my picture can *ruin it*.

He began ticking off potential setbacks:

—A poorly scripted line of dialogue. A hapless delivery. A garish gown. Unflattering lighting. Maudlin music. Any of these bumbled details can turn a carefully crafted romance into claptrap or a heart-wrenching tragedy into a vaudeville farce. And to this list of pitfalls, I add the public reputations of my stars.

David stood and rolled his sleeves a little tighter, his standard cue that he was about to sum up.

—A movie is not a fancy, Miss Ross. It is not an entertainment or a midsummer night's dream. It is not even a mirage. It is something more tenuous, essential, and rare. And it is my job to ensure that it reaches its audience in an utterly uncompromised condition.

He thrust his hand forward and Miss Ross took it.

—We're glad to have you on board, he said.

Then he strode out of the office, yanking the door so soundly behind him that Marcus's suit coat swung on its hanger like a lantern in the wind.

Miss Ross rose from her chair. She didn't rise like David to signal that she'd be summing up. She rose to put Marcus's piles of paper in their proper spots, taking the time to delicately true the edges of each stack with the palms of her hand.

How did it come to this? Marcus found himself wonder-

ing. As a young attorney, he spent a day in court for every day
behind his desk. From season to season, in the upper gallery the
fans would be waved or the sneezes stifled as he rose deliberately
from his chair and walked toward the jury box to face the twelve
of his fellow men who had been summoned to sit in judgment—
each one fashioned in the Lord's image, yet no two alike. It was
for that very moment that he had become a lawyer: that moment
when the citizenry, intent on voicing its innermost concerns and
meting out the full measure of its vengeance or mercy, was still
prepared to listen.

And yet, Marcus had not entered a courtroom in more
than three years.

In fact, half the very documents that were stacked upon
his desk had been drafted to *avert* an appearance in court: stays;
requests for summary judgment; terms of settlement. On top
of the stack that Miss Ross was straightening at that very moment was a motion to dismiss—which had presumably begun
its journey as a tree. Solitary and majestic, that tree had provided
shade to some little patch of America: in a churchyard, perhaps,
or a pasture, or along a bend in the river where Whistling Billy
McGuire had cast his line. And then, after half a century of providing relief from the sun so reliably, this tree had been uncer-
emoniously felled—so that a middle-aged man without a wife or
children sitting in an office a thousand miles away could string
his carefully qualified arguments together end-to-end.

Through words and clauses.

Paragraphs and pages.

Quires.

Reams.

Bales.

In just three years, Marcus must have caused the clearing of ten thousand acres of virgin growth—single handedly stripping the likes of the Ozarks as bare as might five generations of shipbuilders.

How it would have confounded his father to see it—his father, who for more than thirty-eight years served four hundred families six days a week, providing all manner of seed and feedstock by the pound and the bushel and the peck, and who left behind an unlocked iron box with a marriage license, a birth certificate, a balanced bank account, a cancelled mortgage, two pages of outstanding receipts, and a handwritten last will and testament—for a grand total of ten pieces of paper.

A ray of sunlight graced the paper-laden desk. Marcus followed its diagonal trajectory back though the louvered shades, out into the dusk of the whippoorwill's call, beyond Buildings Five and Six, beyond Stages Ten, Eleven, and Twelve to the farthest reaches of the lot where that well-stocked tributary of the Mississippi River flowed without effort or interruption.

Miss Ross politely cleared her throat.

She had resumed her place in her chair and was smiling. It wasn't a smug smile or a cruel one. It was knowing and sympathetic. It was the way his grandmother used to smile whenever he placed her gin card on top of the discard pile.

—Now, where were we . . . ? Marcus ventured a little half-heartedly.

—I believe we were talking about favors and jobs.

—Yes. So we were, Miss Ross. So we were. And what exactly did you have in mind . . .?

—I didn't have anything in mind, Mr. Benton. But as long as you're asking, I suppose I should take some time to think about it.

She stood and offered her hand.

—It was a pleasure meeting you, she said and she seemed like she meant it.

Then she walked to the bookcase to collect her things. But as she was reaching for her hat, she paused to study the head of Caesar. She picked it up and tossed it lightly in one hand. She looked back at Marcus with the same knowing and sympathetic smile. She didn't say anything, but she didn't need to. For the question was implicit: How much does *this* weigh, Mr. Benton?

She returned the bust to its place with unnecessary care and picked up the rod and hat.

—Mr. Selznick on the line for you, said the electronic voice.

Miss Ross joined Marcus in looking at the intercom. Then rather than heading for the door, she came back toward him. She leaned the rod against his desk and dropped the hat on top of his motion to dismiss.

—I think you need these more than I do, she said.

≡ EVE ≡

As far as Eve was concerned, Chester's should have ushered in a brand-new era of city planning. Plunked on a small paved lot on the corner of Pico and Sepulveda, Chester's was a coffee shop in the shape of a giant coffee pot—complete with a ribbon of steam that twisted from its spout twenty four hours a day. Other than a bench bolted to the ground by the Sepulveda curb, there was no place to sit, and there was nothing for sale other than a twelve ounce cup of coffee brewed in cream. As the sign over the cash register made clear, the three ways you could get your coffee at Chester's were sweetened, unsweetened, and somewhere else.

A chatty panhandler once reported to Eve that Chester had come to California as a prospector in the 1880s. This was malarkey, of course, but Eve liked to believe there was some truth to the tale. She could just picture the old goat sitting by his campfire on the banks of a crooked crick, tinkering with the roasting of his beans, the granularity of his grind, the rapidity of his boil—until his brew was without flaw. So when he finally hit pay dirt, rather than recline in a claw-footed tub, he bought this corner, built this pot, and set about doing the only thing the Good Lord had ever intended him to do. And what the Good

Lord intended for others was their own goddamn business.

SURE, AT FIRST GLANCE Chester's style of commerce seemed a little crackers—Eve would give you that. But all you had to do was spend three bucks in an Automat to see that he was onto something. Because when all was said and done, no slinger of hash was going to master the subtleties of a lemon meringue pie *and* a tuna fish sandwich.

But on the corner of Pico and Sepulveda? There was no hint of the half-assed. Not in Chester's paper cup. With its caramel color and smoky aroma, his coffee was incontestably good. Indisputably good. Unassailably, incontrovertibly, indismissably good.

Come to think of it—you could make a similar claim about the donuts at that donut shop in the shape of a donut over on La Cienega!

In fact, if the Mayor of Los Angeles had any sense, he would immediately establish a new ordinance requiring that every purveyor in the city limits sell no more than one item and that he sell it from a shop in the shape of his merchandise. Like orange juice from a great orange orb, or whiskey from a bottle as tall as the Eiffel Tower. With that simple reform in place, thousands of Chesters from across the country would hear the call. They'd pull up stakes, load their wagons, and head west to this city, which not only approved of but applauded their cranky, intolerant artistry.

—One, please, Eve said to the girl in the window. Unsweetened.

—That'll be ten cents.

—Keep the change.

With coffee in hand and a few minutes to spare, Eve crossed

the lot to take up residence on the solitary bench by the curb.

Whenever Eve came to Chester's in the morning or early afternoon, the bench was empty—like those benches you'd see out on the Hoosier highways, covered in dust and dreaming of Greyhound buses. But whenever she came at 5:30 p.m., rain or shine Chester's bench was occupied by a silver-haired banker in a Brooks Brothers suit. Seeing the old banker there on the corner of Pico and Sepulveda had always struck Eve as a little incongruous, even mystifying. But the minute she sat down, she could see why after a hard day's work he chose to come to this spot for one last cup of coffee before heading home: It was a privileged position from which to witness the motley splendor of the commonwealth. For as narrow as the menu was at Chester's, the clientele was just as broad.

Why, at that very moment, a pair of sleeveless Oklahomans fresh off an oil rig were sipping their coffees beside a posse of Mexicali grape pickers. And chatting up the girl at the window was a matinee idol-in-the-making even as the storefront preacher in the secondhand suit standing right behind him waited to place his order with the patience of Job. Denizens and drifters. The fabulous and the fallen. It simply livened the spirits to see so many different kinds of people dedicating a few unspoken-for minutes to life, liberty, and the pursuit of happiness.

Eve leaned back against the bench and took a sip of her coffee thinking that she was certainly going to miss Chester's when she left L.A. And just as her thoughts were shifting to trunks and tickets and the other practicalities of intercontinental travel, as if on cue a dusty black Ford with a stack of luggage strapped to its roof pulled into a parking space a few feet away. Eve watched with interest as the doors flung open and a roly-poly pair of pensioners emerged. Before he could even stretch his back, the husband put his hands on his hips and took in the giant coffee pot from its wide blue base to its tippity top where the wisp of steam trailed toward the heavens unceasingly.

—Now, I've seen everything, he said.

Eve took another sip of her coffee and smiled at sudden thoughts of her great Aunt Polly. Clad in black from head to toe, her needlepoint never far from reach, proper Aunt Polly from Bloomington, Indiana, also liked to let people know when she had seen everything. What was it about that phrase, mused Eve, that made it so popular with those who had no business using it?

It was in the fire-cracking month of July that Aunt Polly and Uncle Jake would pay their yearly visit. And while they stayed, no matter how hellacious the heat, afternoon tea would be served in the sitting room without fail. For Aunt Polly loved afternoon tea as much as she loved Jesus—and it was through constancy that she intended to prove her devotion to both. So, the day before Aunt Polly arrived, Eve's mother would take the fine china from the back of the closet (where it belonged), so that Maisy could sweep the dead flies from the cups. And every afternoon at 2:00, the ladies would convene around the teapot as Eve and her sister were shooed out the kitchen door.

At least until 1928, when Evelyn turned fifteen.

That fateful summer, Aunt Polly announced that henceforth the privilege of tea would be hers. (Naturally, this privilege came with a floral dress, barrettes, and the manners befitting a lady.) Since Alice was only twelve, she was allowed to wear pigtails and overalls and stick out her tongue as she zipped out the door in search of bullfrogs, lizards, and the rest of her kin. While Evelyn, hands on her knees, was left to return the stare of the grandfather clock.

Aunt Polly recognized the infallibility of her Deity in all respects but one: He had made summer days too long. So to complete the perfection of His plan, Aunt Polly was intent upon fending off their influence.

How does one fend off the influence of a summer day? You start by serving tea at two in the afternoon. Then, having thanked the Good Lord for His bounty and passed the biscuits, you talk about relatives long since dead. You make sure to dredge up some story that you've dredged up before (having come to the comforting conclusion that the world will welcome as many dredgings as you can muster.) And when the chitchat flags, rather than adjourn like hummingbirds into the waning wonder of the vernal afternoon, you pick up a magazine.

For Aunt Polly, this was preferably a *Saturday Evening Post* that she had read before. Turning through the pages, she would occasionally stop at a photograph—say, of a short-haired Amelia Earhart preparing to cross the Atlantic by plane—in order to remark with a mix of indignation, wisdom, and finality:

—Now, I've seen everything.

FOR GREAT UNCLE JAKE (a harmless old broker of crop insurance who once shook the hand of Herbert Hoover) the headshaking phrase of choice was *If I had a nickel fer*. As in, *If I had nickel fer every time the papers called for rain.*

So enamored with this phrase was Uncle Jake that an *If I had a nickel fer* might well be the only sentence he uttered over the course of a family meal. Which was all the more striking when you considered that his solitary statement would linger forever unfinished.

For, whatever the recurring circumstance that was to conclude in this unprecedented rain of nickels upon Uncle Jake's head, he just couldn't seem to pin down *how* he'd put his windfall to use: Invest in a new pair of suspenders? Spring for a night on the town? Make a solo flight across the Atlantic, or as far from Aunt Polly as earthly geography would allow? Who could say?

Maybe Herbert Hoover, but not Uncle Jake.

One Sunday supper (after an exceptionally languorous tea), when Uncle Jake happened to observe: *If I had a nickel fer every time I heard Roozyvelt on the radio*, Eve simply couldn't stand it. She couldn't abide it. Not in good Christian conscience.

—What, Uncle Jake? she implored (after dropping her knife and fork on her plate). What is it exactly that you would do, once you had all those goddamn nickels?

Alice opened wide the translucent lids of her amphibian eyes.

—Young lady! said Evelyn's mother, her face as pink as her ham.

And Evelyn's father? He simply looked forlorn.

So, in order to spare him the discomfort of administering a reprimand, Evelyn pushed back her chair and sent herself to her room. But as she climbed the stairs, she smiled to hear Aunt Polly declaim:

—Well, I never!

Now *that*, thought Evelyn, was an expression that Aunt Polly had every reason to make use of.

As Eve finished her coffee, a dark green Packard pulled to the curb and its chauffeur leapt from the driver seat in order to open the passenger door.

—Sorry, Miss Ross, he said. I had to go to three newsstands to find it!

—No problem, Billy. Thanks for running it down.

Once in the car, Billy handed the latest issue of *Gotham* into the back, and Eve made herself comfortable. The lead story was an exposé on the knuckleheads who'd vied to build the tallest skyscraper in the world. The drawing on the cover showed the Empire State Building in a boxing ring with its gloves in the air as the Chrysler Building lay flat on its back—and Sigmund Freud looked on from a ringside seat.

Eve laughed out loud.

That image had Katey's fingerprints all over it!

As Eve turned through advertisements in search of the cover story, Billy gave three quick glances into the rearview mirror.

—Are you headed back soon, Miss Ross?

—What's that, Billy?

—I was just wondering if you're headed back to New York?

—Oh, I'm not much for heading back, Billy.

He gave what looked like a nod of understanding and then he stole another few glances in the mirror, apparently in the mood to converse.

Eve closed her magazine.

—How about you, Billy? How are things down at the Corral?

He pulled himself up by the wheel.

—Jim-dandy, Miss Ross. You know that niche I was telling you about?

—Sure, Billy. I remember.

—Well, I think I found it!

A sandy-haired kid with no idea of how good-looking he was bound to become, Billy was one in a million. The real

McCoy. Having herded cattle with his pa back in West Texas, he had come to L.A. at the age of fifteen with a small-time rodeo and then stumbled into pictures when demand was on the rise for men who could fall off of horses. He was just getting his start, you understand (as he was the first to tell you), but he had already charged with the cavalry across a river, over a hill, and through a canyon on the way to the Alamo and the Battle of Bull Run.

An old-timer named Skilly Skillman had apparently taken Billy under his wing. He's the one who had advised Billy that he needed a niche. Something that would set him apart and get him front and center—right in the crosshairs of the camera. Skillman's route to the close-up had been through the saloon window. Sure, he could tumble down the stairs or get clocked on the noggin with the rest of them. But when it came to being thrown through a window, no one was his equal. He was the undisputed king of defenestrations.

Eve could hardly wait to hear what Billy's route was going to be . . .

—For me, he explained, it's gonna be the heel-hooker.

—The heel-hooker?

Billy nodded with enthusiasm as he veered around a cab.

—That's when you're ridin' at full gallop . . . And you get an arrow in the chest, see . . . And instead of fallin' clear of your horse, the heel of your boot gets hooked in the stirrup . . .

Billy passed his right hand slowly in front of the windshield, as if he could see his body being dragged through the dust toward the setting sun.

Heck. Eve could practically see it too.

—You can't beat a man who's found his niche, Eve admitted with a smile.

—No ma'am, said Billy. I suspect you can't.

Then he gave the rearview mirror a few more glances like he'd just had a notion.

—You know what, Miss Ross? Why don't you come down to the Corral? Then you can see it for yourself!

Now it was Eve who was sitting up.

—That's a hell of an idea, Billy. Why don't you hand me the lists.

Billy leaned to his right, took a pad from the glove compartment, and passed it into the back.

Eve turned to the fourth page—the one which was titled SIGHTS TO SEE BEFORE I LEAVE L.A. Surveying the list from top to bottom and the little green checks that marked her progress, Eve felt a great sense of satisfaction—which, come to think of it, was pretty hilarious when you considered the aversions of her youth.

Eve couldn't pinpoint when her suspicion of lists began, but it must have been early. Maybe as early as seven or eight . . . In the basement of St. Mary's . . . where she and the rest of the second graders memorized the Ten Commandments in Latin as their parents dozed to Father O'Connor upstairs.

Soon after that came the Twelve Apostles with the Thirty Presidents close on their heels. The Seven Deadly Sins. The Five Hundred Rules of Grammar. And that list of all lists: the forever unfurling one that Ol' Saint Nick used to separate the naughty from the nice.

Yep. In Indiana, a young girl had good reason to suspect that lists were the foot soldiers of tyranny—crafted for the sole purpose of bridling the unbridled. A quashing, squashing, squelching of the human spirit by means of itemization.

In search of refuge, at the age of seventeen Eve began stopping in at St. Mary's on the way home from school to light a candle and mutter a prayer. Three months (and sixty nickels) later, Eve's parents actually agreed to send her to Switzerland for a year. They even acted like it was their idea! But when Eve finally arrived at the *académie*, and opened the trunk that had been sent in advance, there on top of a lifetime supply of white buttoned blouses was a handwritten list of *Ten Things a Young Lady Should Remember When Traveling Abroad*.

Naturally, in the heat of the moment this discovery was irksome. But upon reflection, it was the perfect surprise with which to start her excursion. For having smoothed the pleats of her skirt, Eve sat at her desk, corrected her posture, and proceeded to tear her mother's list into five hundred pieces.

Which is actually much harder than it sounds!

The first two hundred tears come rather easy. They're like pulling the drumsticks from a well-roasted turkey. But thereafter, the scraps of paper that you're rending are less than half an inch square. To execute five hundred individual tears requires the delicate finger-work and otherworldly patience of those who scratch the names of angels on the heads of pins.

But, if Eve couldn't identify when her suspicion of lists began, she could remember *exactly* when it ended: She was somewhere in the interminable majesty of the American West, sitting in the dining car of the Golden State Limited, reading a detective novel.

The Crimson Gown . . .

Living up to the promise of its cover, the story began brightly with the strangling of a starlet. In the pages that followed, the nasty particulars of the victim's rise to fame were slowly revealed. Piece by piece the lonely detective puts the sordid puzzle together. But only in chapter nineteen does it finally dawn on him that the hands around the starlet's throat in chapter one had been those of the Oriental chanteuse whom he'd fallen for in chapter five.

In chapter twenty-two, when the detective makes his way to the chanteuse's apartment at one in the morning, she opens the door dressed in the prefigured gown. With a bow, she offers him a chair and pours him a whiskey. He consumes it at one gulp. Then with grim determination, he lays out the elements of the case against her—the primitive means, the engineered opportunity, the convoluted motive. *It's time to go downtown, Baby*, he says at last, and rises to his feet—only to waken eight hours later on the floor of the empty apartment.

Gripping his head, he stumbles down the stairs. In the lobby, he stops to grab the old Chinaman at the desk by his truncated collar, demanding to know where she is.

—She gone, the Chinaman says.

—Gone where?

—Gone back. To Forbidden City . . .

With this news, our hapless shamus reels into the street, headed for the local precinct; or a bar; or maybe a bridge! Eve couldn't say. Because her thoughts, having already ditched the detective, were on the trail of the chanteuse. Having made the journey across the Pacific on a rusty freighter and disembarked on the rickety docks of Shanghai, Eve followed the glamorous fugitive through a pair of intricately carved gates into a maze of gamboled roofs and red lacquered lattice a thousand years old . . .

The Forbidden City, thought Eve. Now, that sounds like a place worth going to!

—Excuse me, she said to the kindly looking stranger across the table. Would you happen to have a pen or pencil handy?

Armed with the stranger's pencil, Eve flipped to the blank page that is always hiding at the end of a book like the unprepared kid at the back of the class. Across the top of the page in large capital letters she wrote PLACES TO GO, and then commenced to itemize:

1.   *The Forbidden City*
2.   *Timbuktu*
3.

After Timbuktu she paused. She bit the pencil's eraser, at a loss for a third locale.

At a loss for a third locale? she chided herself. The world is big. It's bigger than a bread box!

So, Eve closed her eyes and imagined that she was looking down at the earth from the heavens. She watched as the bright blue marble turned so dependably, bringing each continent successively into view. And there, below the parting clouds, a destination presented itself: *Istanbul.* And then another. And another. In fact, so quickly did the destinations come, the kindly stranger's pencil could barely keep up.

3.   *Istanbul*
4.   *Cairo*
5.   *Havana*
6.   *French Polynesia*
7.   *The Taj Mahal!*

Lists aren't so bad, Eve realized. They didn't have to be a catalogue of matronly constraints. They could just as easily testify to plans and intentions. A celebration of the not yet done. Of what *thou shalt.*

It really just depended on which side of the pencil you were on.

On her first night in residence at the Beverly Hills Hotel, Eve asked her waiter if he could spare a pencil and pad. Then under the hotel's palmy moniker, in honor of her proximity to Hollywood, she itemized a list of her favorite improbable motion picture conclusions. The next night (at the Cocoanut Grove), it was a list of the town's dullest leading men. In the nights that followed, as she dined across the city alone, her narrow little pad proved a boon companion. And when fellow hotel resident Prentice Symmons expounded on all the sights that Eve should see before she left L.A., she made a list of those.

That list, originally comprising ten items, was quickly expanded to fifteen; and then to twenty. So in what little space she had left at the bottom of the page, Eve scratched in number twenty-one: *Watch Billy do a Heel-Hooker.* Then she closed her compendium and gave it a satisfied pat, just as Billy was pulling into the visitors' lot.

The lot was bordered with palms—those fantastical trees that seemed to be cultivated everywhere in California despite providing so little in the way of shade. Billy scooted around the car to open Eve's door. As she climbed out, he stood with his posture impressively upright and his gaze fixed on some point in the distance. It must have taken all of his presence of mind not to salute.

—How long will you be, Miss Ross?

—To tell you the truth, Billy, I have no idea. Do you think you can wait?

—You betcha!

Following a prominent path through the palms, Eve soon came upon a clearing in which grazed a small herd of one-story buildings. Eve had been to the studio a few times before in order to visit Olivia on the set, but she had never been to this particular spot. Since there were no signs and the buildings looked identical, Eve figured she'd have to start knocking on doors. But just as she prepared to eeny-meany-miney-moe, from behind one of the buildings came a barefooted boy in a floppy straw hat with a fishing pole propped on his shoulder . . .

CONSTANCY. That was the whole problem with Aunt Polly's worldview. An unflinching unwaveriness was the single trait that she presumed the Good Lord valued over everything else. But all you had to do was answer your telephone once in a while to see that constancy had nothing to do with it.

What God liked most was surprises. He liked up-endings and reversals. Empires that overreached, and fortunes bet on black, and vows of eternal devotion founded on a glance. Maybe it was due to some all-knowing sense of fair play; or maybe, He just got bored. But when it came to the cautious and considered endeavors of men, the Divine was sure to flummox.

How else to make sense of the kindly Marcus Benton and his out-of-the-blue invitation to a tête-à-tête? With his mussed up hair, wrinkled shirt, and vaguely familiar demeanor, Eve was inclined to like him from the start—but she couldn't have guessed in a million years what he wanted.

And if, as Mr. Benton began to lay his cards on the table, Eve had any remaining doubts as to the importance of surprise in the workings of Providence, the Good Lord dispelled them in His inimitable style with the throwing open of a door and the barging in of a latter-day Napoléon.

For despite all the laughs that they had shared over Livvy's stories from the set, Eve hadn't really understood what her friend was up against until the Emperor started talking. With his two-cornered hat on his head and his little hand tucked in his coat, he launched into a zingy description of Hollywood full of fifty-dollar phrases like: *Titanic personalities* and *innermost humanities*. Clearly, he was partial to a full-blown soliloquy, but it didn't take long to get the gist of his message: that his irreplaceable genius was under constant threat from the essential fallibility of those in his employ.

Mr. Benton (who had obviously heard versions of the speech before) let his attention wander toward the rays of light that angled through the window shade. Somewhere outside a bird marked the dwindling day with a warble, which seemed to provide him momentary relief from his employer's oratory, presumably by recalling some afternoon in a distant and more sensible time.

As Napoléon began to elaborate for no one's benefit but his own, Eve felt a surge of sympathy for Mr. Benton. He suddenly had the look of a stranger in his own office. And that's when she realized why his demeanor had seemed so familiar: It was the same as her father's. Sitting behind their well-meaning piles of paper in their well-appointed offices, they both had good reason to let their minds wander.

Napoléon was standing now. He summed up smartly, took Eve's hand, and then disappeared through the door, drawing the curtain on the conversation that he hadn't been invited to in the first place.

WHEN EVE EMERGED from Mr. Benton's office a few minutes later, rather than return to the Packard she headed straight for the back forty to find Olivia on the set. In a few hours they would be meeting for dinner at the Tropicana, but Eve couldn't wait to relay this turn of events. On the rolling lawn that rested grace-fully between the majesty of Tara and its fields in high cotton, Eve would describe her meeting with Napoléon word-for-word, and Livvy would bust her bustle with laughter.

But as Eve came around the corner, she was startled to find the plantation desolate. Overnight, the trees had been up-rooted, the grass singed, the peacocks scattered, and the stables now listed like a ship that had run ashore. Without a living soul in sight, the scene gave an irrefutable impression of abandon-ment. But when Eve crossed the porch and opened the front door, she found the entrance hall teeming with craftsmen.

Standing halfway up the staircase, a young man gen-tly dented the banister with a ball-peen hammer as his colleague scuffed the treads of the steps with a pumice stone. To Eve's left, a lanky technician with an elaborate apparatus on his back—like that of an exterminator—was spraying a tainted liquid onto the bright floral wallpaper to create the impression of water stains, while an-other fellow brushed sepia around a taped-off square to form the ghostly shadow of where a framed work of art once had hung.

Eve passed through the entry into the inner chamber and paused beside a vandalized portrait in order to watch a man in bifocals carefully cracking a mirror with a jeweler's hammer. It was all so breathtaking.

Presumably, Selznick imagined that these technicians worked for him—that they followed his instructions and ful-filled his plan like his fitters and gaffers and grips. But Eve could see in an instant that these were a different class of men. Like the archangels, these artisans had come to dismantle the utmost accomplishments of mortal men. Working with at least as much ingenuity as the finest of engineers, they were slowly undoing what pride and ambition, wealth and tradition had assembled with such self-conscious care.

As Selznick had gone on and on about his professional prowess and the artful execution of his films, Eve's natural inclination had been to dismiss his every word. But, perhaps the megalomaniac had been onto something. Not what he thought he was onto. At least, not exactly. The notion that every little person involved in a picture could ruin it was just plain loony. But maybe there were some—a select few at large among the multitudes—who in the guise of fulfilling the Emperor's plan could actually play an instrumental role in the grander design of the Great Bamboozler.

—We're glad to have you on board, Selznick had said to Eve.

And maybe the feeling was mutual.

Eve turned around and headed back outside onto the lilting porch. Rather appropriately, Selznick had built the O'Hara's plantation house on the highest point of the back forty, and as Eve looked off into the distance, she found herself thrilled by the view. Not by the sun, which was sinking somewhere over the Pacific; nor by the isolated lights in the valley, which had begun to flicker in domestic tranquility. What gave her that tingling feeling was the recognition that for as far as the eye could see, there was no skyline to speak of. No high-rises, no office towers, no bridges imposing themselves upon the horizon.

How different it was from New York, where those tiresome silhouettes incessantly reminded its citizens that theirs was a city built on merit and effort and achievement. Los Angeles wasn't built on any of that, thought Eve with a sense of serenity. It was built on something more tenuous, essential, and rare.

Eve looked at her watch.

It was just after five—too late to join Prentice for tea,

but hours before she was due to meet Livvy at the Tropicana. She wondered if the silver-haired banker was sitting on his bench at Chester's. If she hurried, she just might be able to join him for a cup of coffee and a little conversation before she headed home.

THE END

ABOUT THE AUTHOR

Born and raised in the Boston area, Amor Towles received his BA from Yale College and an MA in English from Stanford University. His first novel, *Rules of Civility*, published in 2011, was a *New York Times* bestseller and was named by the *Wall Street Journal* as one of the best books of 2011. His second novel, *A Gentleman in Moscow*, published in 2016, was on the *New York Times* bestseller list for over a year while in hardcover. It was named as one of the best books of 2016 by the *Chicago Tribune*, the *Washington Post*, the *Philadelphia Inquirer*, the *San Francisco Chronicle*, and NPR. Both novels have been translated into over twenty languages. Having worked as an investment professional for over twenty years, Mr. Towles now devotes himself fulltime to writing in Manhattan, where he lives with his wife and two children.

For more information visit amortowles.com